C000085507

Under the Orange Trees

Copyright © by Akin Yilmaz

Edited by Lucy Neame

ISBN 9798 3700 15434

Dedicated to my father, Yilmaz Mehmet.

ONE

The terminal building at Nicosia International Airport was like a fortress. Troops from the Lancashire Fusiliers patrolled the parameter of the airport checking all vehicles that entered. Once in the terminal all persons and any items of luggage, bags, etc. were searched by officers of the police mobile reserve. Ali Mustafa causally walked towards the arrivals gate when he suddenly stopped outside a newspaper kiosk. A photo of a man on the front cover of the Cyprus Mail was responsible for this. Ali picked up the paper and stared at the front page. Panayotis Michalis was a member of EOKA and was the main suspect in the murder of a Policeman in the village of Tera. The same village Ali was from. Seen in the neighbouring village of Arodes by police, Michalis tried to run before being shot and killed. Ali carefully placed the newspaper on top of the pile.

Flight number 2212 from London had just landed and Ali stood opposite the arrivals gate waiting for his son, his mind still preoccupied by the image of Michalis. He never knew or met Michalis, but he did know the policeman that Michalis killed, Sergeant Hasan Mustafa, Ali's brother. People surged forward as the arrival gate opened sweeping Ali with them until he was pinned against the metal barrier. He put his arms on the barrier and forcefully pushed back his body before turning his head around and giving everyone a look of disdain. Passengers started arriving through the gate and not too long after Ali raised his hand to acknowledge seeing his son.

Kaya Mustafa was carrying two large cases and was wearing a white shirt with the coat of arms of Cambridge University on the front. The pair hugged.

'Welcome home son,' Ali said softly.

Ali took the cases and walked ahead; Kaya sensed something was wrong.

'Well, how did you do?' asked Ali.

A smile appeared on Kaya's face.

'Dad, Stop!'

Ali put both pieces of luggage down. Kaya rummaged around in his trouser pocket before producing a brown envelope. He took out a letter and handed it to his dad. Ali opened it up before a puzzled expression took shape.

'I don't understand it,' Ali said.

Kaya pointed to a sentence written in the letter.

'First class honours in Archaeology,' whispered Ali.

'First class!' he then shouted out startling the people around them.

'My son has a first class degree from Cambridge,' he shouted out a few decibels louder.

Ali and Kay smiled as they left the terminal as the eyes of several British soldiers followed them to Ali's truck. The sense of jubilation departed Ali's face as they got into the truck and drove into the queue to wait for the soldiers to open the car park barrier before they could leave the airport.

'What's wrong Dad?' asked Kaya.

'Your Uncle Hasan is dead.'

'No!' Kaya said grabbing his father's arm.

The soldiers opened the car park barrier and Ali sped off leaving the soldiers covered in dust.

'When, how did he die?'

'EOKA murdered him,' Ali said in a matter-of-fact way.

'Two days ago your Uncle was sitting outside the village café when two terrorists rode by on a motorbike. One of them walked up and shot him. The next day the police found the bike and waited for the two terrorists. After a gun fight and both terrorists were shot and one died,' explained Ali trying in vain to show no emotion.

'When's his funeral?'

'Tomorrow morning. We wanted to bury him today but the police are not releasing his body until this afternoon. The ceremony will be at the mosque in Polis before we drive him to Terra for burial,' Ali confirmed.

Kaya stared into the road ahead finding it difficult to digest the information his father had told him.

Nicosia to Tera was approximately a one a half hour journey but the silence in the car made it feel much longer.

'Can I help carry uncle's coffin?' asked Kaya.

Ali slowly shook his head.

'Four of his police colleagues, Uncle Saban and me will be carrying the coffin.'

A heavy army and police presence was visible as the truck approached Tera. Farmers waved at Kaya and his father as they entered the village. Kaya's mother, Nalan, eagerly waited outside the house.

'He's here,' she shouted.

This prompted his elder sister, Melis and younger brother, Enver, to rush out of the house, Enver was trying to put his shirt on but kept missing the sleeve opening.

'My boy, my boy,' Nalan kept saying.

As Kaya stepped out of the car he was overwhelmed by

his mother.

'Leave the boy alone,' Ali said while lifting Kaya's luggage out of the truck.

'How did you do?' Nalan asked Kaya.

'I will tell you inside,' Kaya said as he embraced his brother and sister.

For a brief period happiness shone in the house as Kaya told his mother and siblings of his amazing academic achievement. Ali didn't share in the happiness keeping himself busy by attending to the goats on his farm.

Howls of crying enveloped the inside of Polis Mosque encircling the open coffin of Sergeant Hasan. Kaya looked around trying to calculate the number of people that were crammed into the mosque to bid farewell to his uncle. One of the saddest sights Kaya witnessed was his three little cousins holding hands whilst standing next to the coffin transfixed by the body of their father. The Imam walked up to the coffin and recited several Islamic prayers. The six pallbearers, Ali, Saban, Sergents Yilmaz, Ali, Ferdi and Officer Suleiman, stood behind the coffin and the Imam gestured for the coffin to be closed and sealed and announced that those people who wished to pray should make their way to the prayer hall, which had a separated area for women. The pallbearers lifted the coffin and carried it outside and down the guard of honour, formed by all offices of Hasan's police unit. All the officers gave salute, as the coffin was placed on a horse drawn carriage. Family and friends got into cars to follow the carriage to Tera, where Hasan would be buried.

Tera cemetery was on the outskirts of the village and going by the relatively few graves, it had only been built a few years before hand. Four British soldiers circled the perimeter wall of the cemetery as they caught sight of the funeral procession arriving. Every man, woman, child, and dog from the village seemed to be in attendance. A soldier stood guard at the cemetery entrance checking the villagers as they entered. The carriage stopped outside, and Ali and Saban waited for the others to arrive. The police unit arrived, and the four officers joined the brothers in lifting the coffin from the carriage and carrying it into the cemetery, before carefully lowering it into the grave. The officers joined their unit who had lined up behind the Imam. After he uttered some blessings, the mourners were invited to grab a handful of soil and throw it into the grave onto Hassan's coffin before making their way out of the cemetery. Kaya stood by his family as Sergeant Yilmaz approached them, he was one of Hasan's closest friends and both signed up to the police force at the same time. Yilmaz embraced Kaya's mother and father before turning to embrace him and kiss him on both cheeks.

'Kaya, I would not have recognized you if I saw you alone on the street. How was Cambridge University?'

'It was good Yilmaz Abi. I got a first-class degree,' Kaya said in a shy voice.

'Wonderful! You must be proud of him Ali?' Yilmaz said turning his head to Ali.

Ali nodded.

Yilmaz said his farewells and walked towards his unit. Ali nudged Kaya in the arm and raised his finger at Yilmaz.

'He is the policeman who shot Michalis.'

The roar of a motorcycle engine woke Kaya up from his deep dream. In the land of the Pharaohs, he and his team had discovered a tomb near Alexandria. All empirical evidence had led Kaya to believe that the tomb dated back to around 450 - 500 BC, the time of the 27th dynasty during which time Egypt was part of the Persian Empire, but as he entered the darkened room and turned on his flashlight a glistening object reflected to him momentarily blinding him. The object in question was a full-length stature of a man. Kaya touched it; it was cold, and it was also gold. Touching the face, he was confused by the familiarity of the statue's features. Suddenly he stood back and shone the light on its face. It was Alexander the Great.

'Kaya, it's the postman he has a letter for you,' shouted his Mum from downstairs.

Opening the wooden shutters, he just about glimpsed the motorcycle disappearing in a cloud of dust. Not many people received letters in the village and Kaya felt a certain tint of privilege. Nalan handed him the letter and using a knife he slowly and carefully cut open the top of the envelope with the precision of a surgeon.

'Who's it from?' Nalan enquired.

Kaya took a moment to read it and another to re-read it.

'It's from Mr Megaw.'

'Who?' said Nalan with a screwed-up face.

Kaya clinched his fist in triumph.

'Peter Megaw is the director of the Department of Antiquities, and he has invited me for an interview,' he said in a monotone voice of disbelief.

'What interview?' Nalan blurted out.

'There is a vacancy for a role of technician at the archaeological survey branch and they want me to go to Lefkosa for an interview,' explained Kaya, but Nalan could not comprehend a word he had said.

'I have to tell Dad.'

Kaya rushed out the house waiving the letter in his hand. Ali was collecting freshly laid eggs from the newly built chicken coop at the side of the house.

'Dad, I have an interview,' Kaya shouted out.

Ali raised his arm in acknowledgement.

'Next Monday at the Department of Antiquities in Lefkosa,' Kaya said unable to contain his happiness.

'What time next Monday?' Ali asked rubbing his dirty hands onto his overalls.

'Ten o'clock.'

'I'll take you. I need to see someone there so that is very good timing,' Ali said as he took the letter from Kaya to read it.

'This is the perfect job for you.'

'Why do you think I am so happy?' Stated Kaya.

'That is good, but the interview is next Monday so until then you can help me with some farm work,' Ali said handing the letter back to his son.

It proved to be a long day helping his Father on the farm, but as he headed towards the house from the fields he saw his father talking to two men at the front of the house. Kaya did not recognize either of the men and when they noticed Kaya the two men left with haste.

'Who are those men?' Kaya asked his father.

'Buyers. They want some oranges and lemons, so I directed them to Mehmet Bey's house,' Ali told his son.

Curious by nature, Kaya walked into the road, and he could see the two men seated in a land rover staring at what looked like a map. Pretending to check the tyres of his father's truck, he kept his eyes on the men until they finally drove off some few minutes later.

Monday morning had crept up on Kaya as he dipped his mum's freshly baked bread into the bowl of pekmez being careful not to drip any on his prized

Cambridge University shirt. Pekmez was one of his favourite dishes for breakfast, made from carob grown on his father's farm. Ali entered the kitchen.

'We need to leave now, or you'll be late for your interview,' Ali barked out.

As Kaya got up from the chair some pekmez dripped onto his shirt, unaware of this he rushed out of the house to catch up with his father who was already in the truck starting the engine.

'Good luck Kaya,' his mother shouted out.

'My case!' Kaya shouted out as he ran back into the house to fetch his briefcase.

Before Kaya had a chance to close the car door Ali put his foot down and the truck accelerated away.

A group of British soldiers stood on the roadside visually checking all vehicles traveling in and out of the village.

'I hope they don't pull us over,' Ali said as they approached the soldiers. One of the soldiers waved them on.

'Where will you be based if you get the Job?' asked Ali.

'It could be anywhere on the Island. Wherever they decide to start excavations. The main site is in Salamis, but they may want to start excavations elsewhere. I know they want to start excavations in and around Paphos,' explained Kaya.

Even at ten o'clock in the morning Nicosia was hot and humid. The truck headed towards the old venetian walls and Paphos Gate before turning right on to Museum Road. Ali parked outside the Cyprus Museum.

'Oh, you've had a slight accident,' Ali said pointing to Kaya's shirt.

Two brown stains caused by the pekmez were clearly visible on the pristine white shirt.

8

'How am I going to clear it off?' said Kaya in a stressed voice.

'If you try cleaning it with a damp cloth it will smudge and make it look worse. I would just cross my arms so it's not too visible,' Ali suggested.

'I have no other choice,' Kaya said stepping out of the truck with his briefcase.

'I am going to be at the buyuk han. When you have finished come and find me there. Good luck,' Ali told his son.

Two policemen stood at the entrance of the museum. 'What have you got in the case?' asked one of the policemen.

'Papers, just some papers. I have an interview with Mr Megaw.' Kaya informed the policemen.

'Open the case.'

'I promise just papers,' Kaya said.

'Open it,' insisted the policeman.

Kaya opened it and took out various papers, but a sudden gust of wind blew the papers out of his hand and all over the steps leading up to the entrance. The policemen laughed as Kaya ran around collecting the papers.

Mr Megaw's office was palatial with artefacts scattered around making it akin to an exhibition room. He was sat at his desk as his secretary showed in Kaya.

'Ah, Mr Mustafa take a seat. Please join me I have what you Cypriots call Pekmez.'

'Thank you Sir, but I have already had some,' Kaya said pointing to the stains on his shirts. Megaw laughed.

'It happens to me all the time. I always keep a couple of spare shirts in the office,' confessed Megaw as he sat down behind his desk.

Megaw skim read the letter that was on his desk. Kaya instantly recognized the scruffy handwriting as his.

'So you went to Peterhouse,' said Megaw

'Yes sir.'

'I read architecture at Peterhouse a long time ago, a quarter of a century ago to be precise. A very impressive letter. Who was your Professor at Cambridge?' Megaw asked.

Kaya delved into his brief case and produced a typed letter on Cambridge University headed paper.

'This is a letter from Professor Alwright, my head tutor,' he said handing the letter to Megaw.

Megaw nodded his head with great enthusiasm as he read the letter.

'Yes, I remember Alwright, how is the old boy?'

'He is doing well, a great tutor and mentor, without him I would not have been able to gain a first.'

'I think Mr Mustafa we may well have a role for you. As you may know we established the archaeological survey branch two years ago and we are eager to expand the number of excavations on the island, but Mr Catling, the head of the branch has a particular project in mind for you,' Megaw explained. Kaya was all ears.

'Come with me, let me introduce you to Mr Catling.'

Megaw leapt from his chair.

'Follow me.'

Kaya quickly closed his brief case and followed Megaw out of the office, finding it hard to keep up with Megaw who was travelling down the corridor and breakneck speed. Megaw knocked on a door and entered the office of Hector Catling, head of the Archaeological Survey Branch, Kaya followed in. Catling was caught unaware of this sudden invasion and rapidly folded the newspaper he was reading.

'Mr Catling this is Mr Mustafa.'

Catling and Kaya shook hands.

'Pleased to meet you Mr Catling,' said Kaya nervously.

'Right, I am going to leave you in Mr Catling's capable hands, and he will explain everything. Anyway, it was a pleasure meeting you Mr Mustafa and I am certain our paths will cross again.' And with that Megaw shook Kaya's hand.

'Oh, Mr Catling I have Mr Mustafa's papers in my office so pop by afterwards to collect them,' said Megaw as he left the room.

'Please take a seat. I am not sure how much Mr Megaw explained, but we are planning a number of excavations. We have started a dig at Paphos and there is another site near your village Tera. Remains of an old Roman fort dating back to the second century AD were found many years ago but no excavations have ever taken place. Since, you have experience of leading a dig in Egypt, the branch would like you to lead on excavating the site. We will assign two assistants and for the first few weeks, Mr Kyriacos Nicolaou, my assistant would visit the site a couple times a week to see how things are coming along. You will be reporting to Mr Nicolaou. What are your first thoughts?' Catling asked Kaya.

'I did not expect to lead an excavation in my first role,' said a surprised Kaya.

'I must emphasis that it is only a small site, but maybe ideal for someone leading a dig for the first time,' said Catling.

'Yes, I would be a very happy man if you gave me an opportunity to lead this.'

'Good man,' said catling as he shook Kaya's hand.

'When do I start?' Kaya asked.

'We have some formalities to do first, contracts and all

that. But once we have completed these you can start immediately. We will arrange a day next week you can come and I will introduce you to Mr Nicolaou and your two assistants. Your title will be an archaeological technician.'

Cloud nine was a familiar setting for Kaya. He reached it the first time round when he graduated from Cambridge, and now he was surfing them clouds again. Wandering the streets, he walked under a sign showing Nicosia in English, Lefkosia in Greek alphabet and Lefkosa in Turkish and turned into Ledra Street. The street was nicknamed 'murder mile' due to the number of British Soldiers, policeman and civilians murdered along the street. An open top Land Rover with four British soldiers slowly drove by, Kaya gave them a brief glance before continuing on his way before approaching the imposing Buyuk Han. The Great Inn was built by the Ottomans during the sixteenth century and down the centuries it had been an inn frequented by merchants from Turkey and even a prison under the British. It was now being used as a refuge for poor families where they could rent rooms at affordable prices. Kaya stood by the entrance looking around for his father. Opposite the Buyuk Han was a market and through the crowd he spotted his father. Starting to walk towards him, Kaya suddenly stopped. Standing next to and talking to Ali were two men. Recognizing the two men as the ones he saw with Ali in the village, Kaya stepped behind a goods van so he wouldn't be seen. Ali had told him that the men were interested in buying oranges and lemons and he had re-directed them to see someone else. So, if that was the case why was he meeting them again? Kaya bided his time behind the vehicle while a couple of men unloaded crates of Keo beer bottles. Ali shook the hands of the two men and walked across the street to find Kaya.

'How was the interview?' Ali asked.

'Dad, they want me to lead an excavation team at the old roman camp.'

'You are brilliant,' Ali said giving his son a manly hug. 'When do you start?'

'I am coming back next Wednesday to meet the team and make final arrangements. It is only a small site, but if I can prove that I can manage a team they may send me to the Paphos dig,' said Kaya with great excitement.

'Come on let's go for something to eat and you can tell me all about it,' Ali said putting his arm around Kaya.

On their return to Tera Sergeant Yilmaz was waiting for them inside the house. Ali was clearly apprehensive when he saw Yilmaz.

'Kaya how did the interview go?' asked Yilmaz.

'I have been made an offer to lead an excavation of the old Roman army fort outside Tera,' Kaya said with all the enthusiasm in the world.

'The ruins near Kritou Tera. We received a call last year that some people had been spotted digging there, so a

couple of officers had to go tell them to stop. People say there is Roman treasure near Tera, but no one has ever reported finding anything,' commented Yilmaz.

'Yes, my grandfather always used to say there's gold in the hills,' said Ali.

'Congratulations Kaya and good luck. The reason I'm here is to inform you that we have detained two more terrorists that were part of the cell led by Michalis. We believe that is all the members of the group,' confirmed Yilmaz.

'I heard there were seven or eight in that terrorist unit and including Michalis you've counted four,' Ali retorted back.

'If you know who the others are tell me then,' snapped back Yilmaz.

'As I said it is what have heard,' Ali said slowly.

'These men murdered your brother so if you hear anything you need to inform the police.'

'What is the worst that can happen to them?' Ali asked.

'What do you mean?' Yilmaz said confused.

'Take the example of Sampson. How many soldiers and policemen has he killed 15 or 16? He's been arrested and yes, they may send him to prison in Britain, but what happens when the British decide to leave Cyprus. It will be sooner rather than later. All these so-called political prisoners, terrorists, what is going to happen to them? They will be released and become free men again. That is what is going to happen,' Ali said with great conviction.

'I do not know what is going to happen Ali, but if you hear anything you must tell me,' Yilmaz said as he got up. 'Anyway, I must go. Well done again Kaya.' Yilmaz left.

The conversation made Kaya wonder about what his father had said and whether he knew more than he was letting on.

Time seemed to crawl painfully along for Kaya during the next few days but once he opened his eyes and it was Wednesday morning things began to speed up.

'Kaya, what would you like for breakfast today,' Nalan yelled through the house.

'Anything but pekmez,' shouted back Kaya.

Ali's truck somehow had an extra gear or two and to Kaya the journey to Lefkosa took half the time than the week before.

'I'll wait for you in the café opposite the market,' Ali told

Kaya.

Instead of a stain caused by pekmez this time Kaya's shirt carried stains of sweat. Waiting in reception of the Museum he noticed a case cabinet containing fragments of pottery dating from the time of Alexander the Great. Two men approached him, he recognized Catling but not the other man.

'Mr Mustafa, I would like to introduce you to Kyriacos Nicolaou. You will report directly to him. He will initially come with to carry out a site survey and once this is completed and signed off the excavations can begin. Mr Nicolaou will be the site director and you will be site manager.' Catling explained.

The men walked through a labyrinth of corridors before entering a large room with two people sat around desks.

'After the site survey is complete and the excavations begin, I will come down once a week normally on a Friday and you can give me a report and show me any findings the team has discovered,' stated Nicolaou.

Catling bid farewell and left the room.

'Let me introduce you to your team. This is Andrea.'

Andrea stood up and shook Kaya's hand. She had short brown hair and piercing green eyes that went right through him.

'Andrea has been with us since the survey branch was established two years ago.'

'Welcome on board,' Andrea said with a broad smile.

'And this is Christos.'

Christos reluctantly stood up and shook Kaya's hand. A far colder reception then he received from Andrea.

'Andrea and Christos met whilst both studying archaeology at Athens university. Kaya gained a first-class degree from Cambridge University,' Nicolaou informed them.

'So, you graduated from Cambridge?' Christos asked rhetorically.

'Yes,' Kaya answered to make a point.

'Well done, you must be a smart man,' added Christos.

Kaya just nodded in the hope of killing the conversation.

'Kaya and I will be carrying out a site survey of the Roman fort next week. Once the survey is completed, we can begin the dig,' confirmed Nicolaou.

'Mr Nicolaou, can I please ask a question?' asked Christos

'Of course.'

'Why do we require three people to excavate such a small site?' asked Christos.

'Simple, the more people we have the less time we spend there. In my opinion I tend to agree with you Christos, I do not think the time and resources we will spend on this site is worth it. I do not think we will find anything of any historical significance there,' confessed Nicolaou.

'Then, why are we excavating there?' asked a confused Kaya.

'The British hope to find some Roman artefacts they can then send back to the British Museum. I apologise for my negative thoughts but the whole idea of setting up the Archaeological Survey Branch is to plunder more treasures for Britain,' Nicolaou expressed.

'Anything of significance that is discovered would be put on display here in this museum,' countered Kaya.

Nicolaou and Christos smirked at each other.

'Well let us wait and see, hopefully we can find something of value and significance,' said Nicolaou.

TWO

Dawn was an amazing sight from the Roman fort near Tera. From the east the peaks of the Troodos mountains framed the picturesque view and to the North the sunlight reflected from the sea at Chrysochou Bay almost blinding Kaya who was observing through binoculars.

'Such a beautiful view,' commented Nicolaou.

'It sure is,' reaffirmed Kaya.

Kaya handed the binoculars to Nicolaou before sitting down on the ground to continue drawing the site map of the area. Nicolaou peeked over Kaya's shoulder to view the map nodding his head in approval.

'Very good depiction of the site. I am afraid my drawing capabilities fall far short of yours,' Nicolaou said as he stepped onto the stones that once formed the roman observation tower and started looking through the binoculars. He pointed into the distance.

'I can see the army camp at Limni.'

'Yes, you can actually follow the road from the camp to Tera,' stated Kaya.

'The Romans would have had a great view of the port of Arsinoe. In fact, every approach to the fort would have been seen. Who owns the land on the hillside just outside your village?' Nicolaou asked.

'Where?' Kaya asked as he stood up and took the binoculars from Nicolaou.

'The land over there covered by trees,' specified Nicolaou.

'The land belongs to Mehmet Bey. They are lemon and orange trees, below there past the stream are olive groves, which have been there for centuries. They were probably there during the Roman times,' explained Kaya.

Kaya walked around the ruins.

'So, these walls were the outer perimeter of the fort and these stones formed the inner courtyard and over there was the main building,' Kaya explained to Nicolaou while simultaneously trying to show him on his hand drawn map.

Nicolaou noticed something in the undergrowth. He put on his gloves and pulled out the nettles and weeds to reveal a stone slab.

'What is it?' asked Kaya.

'I can make out some writing,' responded Nicolaou.

Kaya poured water onto the stone from his container and Nicolaou used his glove to scrub the earth and other particles off it.

'Can you read it?' Nicolaou asked Kaya.

Kaya read the writing.

'Present here is Gaius Calpurnius Flaccus to honour the life of Lucius Octavis, Legatus Augusti Pro Prartore, who died near here,' Kaya read out.

'Flaccus was the Roman Governor of Cyprus in about 122 or 123 AD, but I have never heard of Lucius Octavis,' said Nicolaou.

'There is more writing further down the stone, but I would need to clean it more,' Kaya said scrubbing the stone with the bare palms of his hands.

'This is good. I have never made a discovery like this on the first day of a site inspection,' admitted Nicolaou.

'I will clean up the stone later. Mr Nicolaou, I have finished drafting the site map,' Kaya said handing over the sheet of paper.

'Very good. I will take this back to the museum and get some prints. Can I give you a lift back to your village?'

'No, I will stay here a bit longer and try and decipher the writing on that stone. I will walk back to Tera,' said a very excited Kaya.

'In that case, I will leave now. I will inform Christos and Andrea to come here from next Monday.'

'Well, that will give me four days to prepare the site for the main excavation work to begin,' Kaya told Nicolaou.

'Good, I will probably make a visit in two weeks then,' Nicolaou said shaking Kaya's hand before getting into his Land Rover and driving off through the dirt track before finding the road. Kaya rummaged around in his bag before producing a trowel and brush. He knelt and began brushing away the dirt from the stone that had the inscription written on it. Placing a large sheet of paper onto the stone he used a piece of charcoal to rub over the paper until the letters of the inscription were transferred onto the paper. Using two sheets of paper he was able to transfer the whole inscription.

Nalan had prepared Bean stew and freshly baked bread to soak up the juices of the beans, onions, and tomatoes. That was Kaya's favourite part of the meal dipping the bread into the juices.

'How was your first day on site?' Ali asked Kaya across the dining table.

'We found a stone that had a written inscription on it. It probably dates from 123 AD.'

'Wonderful, if you found that on the first day imagine what you will find when you start digging,' commented Ali.

Kaya nodded in agreement as Nalan served more stew into his bowl.

'You must eat well if you are going to spend all day digging,' said Nalan.

Later, Kaya turned on the oil lamp in his bedroom and took out the two sheets of paper with the charcoal inscription before piecing them together and placing it next to a pocket edition of a Cambridge University English – Latin dictionary. He then began the laborious task of deciphering and translating the Latin text into an English transcript. Rubbing his eyes, he glanced at his watch and then did a double take when he realised it was nearly three o'clock in the morning. But the satisfaction was etched on his face as he read the transcript of the inscription on the Roman stone:

Present here is Gaius Calpurnius Flaccus to honour the life of Lucius Octavis, Legatus Augusti Pro Prartore, who died near here on the hill side above the stream in an accidental fall. The brave soldiers of the legion attempted to save his life but to no avail. The Emperor of Rome, Hadrian proclaims Lucius Octavis a great friend and countryman and as a tribute the aureus of Hadrain shall remain in the place of his death to honour his life.

Kaya re-read the transcript and realised that aureus was the gold coins used as currency throughout the Roman Empire at the time. He also underlined *'hill side above the stream.'*

The morning chorus from the cockerels hastened Kaya's departure from home and the journey to the Roman site. He cut through Mehmet Bey's land and followed the stream until he reached the point at the bottom of the hill side. Wading through the stream he began the climb up the hill, weaving in and out of the lemon and orange trees. What the climb proved was that he was unfit. Huffing and puffing as he reached the top of the hill. Debris of fallen rocks lay everywhere but he could make out a narrow pathway. Using his binoculars, he scanned the area until he spotted the ruins of the fort. Clearing the stones away from the path using his boots he followed it until he reached a sharp turn. The path led towards the mountains. Kaya looked down the slope of the hill to the stream below. He sat down on the hill side edge and took out his drawing pad and began to sketch the area around him and every so often he used the binoculars to judge distances. Kaya held up his sketched map and compared it to the real view and stood up with a satisfied look, but as he bent down to pick up his bag, he somehow lost his footing and went tumbling over the side of the hill. So steep was the hill that he could not stop himself rolling further and further down until his head collided with a trunk of an orange tree.

For a moment he lost consciousness and placing his hand on his head he felt a large bump but fortunately there was no blood. Gingerly, he got to his feet and stumbled for a spilt second then he took a couple of steps towards the stream which was only a few feet away. Splashing the cold water on his face. Rejuvenated, Kaya grew frustrated when he turned around to see the contents of his bag strewn down the hill side. Warily he trundled up the hill to collect his belongings, occasionally holding his right side that was giving him great pain. Retrieving his binoculars, trowel and brush he found his bag halfway down the hill, but there was no sign of the paper with his sketched drawing of the area. After a while the pain in his side got the better of him and he slumped down. In the corner of his eye he saw a white flash and he turned to see the sheet of paper plastered onto the truck of a tree and he delicately crawled over to rescue it. He noticed that the root of the tree had grown to such an extent that the ground at base had risen and was protruding out the ground where he saw an object. Kaya used his hands to dig it out, and closer examination showed that it was a small metal fragment, maybe a small bolt or nail. He used the trowel to carve an X on two sides of the tree.

Kaya was still in agony as Doctor Aziz entered his bedroom.

'I hear you have been rolling down hills,' said the Doctor with tongue and cheek.

Kaya didn't see the funny side of his comment.

'Lift your shirt up,' ordered the Doctor.

Kaya's side was bruised. The Doctor touched the area of the bruising and took out his stethoscope placing it on Kaya's back and side.

'You are fine apart from a few bruised ribs. You should take it easy for a week or so and everything will heal naturally, and no tumbling down hills. What were you doing there in the first place?'

'I am starting to excavate the Roman fort and I was drawing a map of the area and I lost my footing and fell,' Kaya explained.

'You know the land you fell down belongs to Mehmet Bay. He once found a roman coin on that hill. If I was you, I would go and speak to him.'

The Doctor's comment perked Kaya up. Nalan entered the room with a bowl of vegetable soup on a tray.

'How is he?' asked Nalan.

'A couple of days bed rest and he'll be fine. That smells so nice,' the Doctor said.

'Shall I serve you a bowl Doctor?'

'No, I have to visit Sergeant Yilmaz's wife.'

'When is she due to give birth?' Asked Nalan.

'Next January, but they are moving to Polis tomorrow, so I want to see her before they leave,' explained the Doctor as he packed his bag.

Later that day Kaya managed to get carefully get dressed and make his way the short distance to Mehmet Bay's house. Mehmet Bay was sitting in the shade avoiding the blistering midday sun. Kaya approached him with some trepidation. Mehmet Bay was a straight-talking, no-nonsense type of man, who commanded the utmost respect within the village.

'Mehmet Bay, sorry to disturb you, but do you have a few minutes to talk to me?' Kaya asked nervously.

Mehmet Bay slightly lifted his hat and looked up at him.

'You are that boy Kaya.'

'Yes sir.'

'Are you feeling better?'

'Yes sir.'

'What were you doing snooping around on my land anyway?' Mehmet Bay asked with a sudden change in the tone of his voice.

'I was on the hilltop before I fell, so I had no intention of going onto your land,' Kaya said in his defense.

'Yilmaz tells me you went to a top university in England, and you are an archaeologist.'

'That is correct, Mehmet Bay.'

'What kind of a job is an archaeologist?' Mehmet Bay asked rhetorically.

'I enjoy it and that is the reason I am here. I was speaking with Doctor Aziz and he mentioned that you once found a Roman coin on your land.'

Mehmet Bay gave Kaya an intense stare.

'Why is the Doctor talking about me?'

'No, we were taking about the ruins of the Roman fort that we are starting to excavate, and the Doctor just mentioned that you had found a Roman coin. I was wondering if you still had it and if I could see it?'

'Why, do you want to take it and put it in one of those museums?' fired back Mehmet Bay.

'Not at all, I just want to see it. I believe there could be more.'

'More!'

'Maybe. If you can remember where you found it.'

'I can remember the exact spot,' Mehmet Bay said in a more engaging fashion.

'Whenever you are free, if you could show me where you found the coin?'

'Wait here,' Mehmet Bay told Kaya as he got up and briskly walked inside his house.

Kaya felt his side that was still giving him pain. Mehmet Bay returned holding a white handkerchief and placed it on a small table before unfolding it and revealing a bright sparkling coin.

'Can I hold it?' asked Kaya.

'Yes, go ahead.'

Kaya picked up the coin and instantly recognized the head of Hadrian facing on the side.

'I would say this coin is over 1800 years old,' confirmed Kaya.

'How much is it worth?' eagerly asked Mehmet Bay.

'I do not know Mehmet Bay. You would have to speak to a coin expert. So, do you remember where you found it?'

'Come with me.' Mehmet Bay said grabbing his tall walking stick and walking off.

Kaya had to walk at a fast pace to keep up with Mehmet Bay who was motoring through the fields. They then crossed a narrow foot bridge across the stream.

'For over two hundred years this land has belonged to my family. There used to be olive trees on this land until they were infected by disease and died. If you look over there you can still see the few that survived.' Mehmet Bay explained.

He then suddenly stopped.

'Here,' he said pointing to a piece of wood sticking out the ground. 'This is the exact spot I found the coin almost twenty years ago.'

Kaya looked around before pointing to the tree that he had carved the crosses on after he had found the small metal piece. He took out the metal item from his pocket and showed Mehmet Bay.

'I found this next to the tree over there,' said Kaya.

'What is it?'

'Probably a nail or bolt used on a cart or carriage dating back from the Roman times.'

'You think there may be more coins in this area?' asked Mehmet Bay.

'Yes, right here,' Kaya confidently said stamping his foot down.

A heron was perched on one of the Roman stones. Andrea tiptoed towards it trying to get a closer view of this tall, elegant bird. She stumbled and this alerted the heron, taking a brief glance in Andrea's direction the startled bird flew off. Christos was watching the British Army camp at Limni through the binoculars.

'A patrol has just left the camp,' announced Christos.

'Why are you so fascinated with the camp? Since you

arrived this morning you have spent half the time watching the camp,' said an annoyed Kaya.

'Sorry sir,' Christos said sarcastically giving an army salute and putting the binoculars down.

Andrea stood over the inscribed stone reading Kaya's transcript.

'What is the meaning of the last sentence about 'as a tribute the aureus of Hadrian shall remain in the place of his death to honour his life?' She asked.

Kaya showed her the dirty map of the hillside.

'I believe this is where the gold aureus coins are buried beneath the citrus groves,' Kaya said pointing to the map before pointing in the direction of the trees.

'Treasure!' shouted Christos.

'Mehmet Bay showed me a coin with Hadrian's head on it that he found some twenty years ago.'

'How many coins do you think could be buried there?' Asked Christos.

'I have no idea. But it mentions a tribute, so it was probably more than one or two,' replied Kaya.

'Did you ask Mehmet Bay if we could dig there?' Andrea asked.

'Technically, we are here to excavate this site and not someone's private land. So that is our main priority, but if we wish to conduct some extracurricular activities there is nothing stopping us,' Kaya confirmed bringing a smile to the faces of all three.

After a couple of hours of digging the intense sun and heat got the better of them and the three sat in the shade under a tree. Kaya opened a basket and offered Andrea and Christos some bread, halloumi and a slice of watermelon.

'Why is this watermelon so sweet? It is delicious,'

proclaimed Andrea as she took another bite.

Kaya was writing in the site logbook.

'Today, so far, the total number of objects found, zero. I think we will give it two more hours and then head on to Mehmet Bay's land for some extracurricular activity,' said Kaya.

Two hours past and still nothing of note had been discovered.

'Come on let's pack up for the day,' shouted Kaya.

All equipment was packed in bags and stored in the boot of the land rover. Christos had one last view of the British army camp through the binoculars before getting into the driver's seat.

'What is the best route to get to Mehmet Bay's land?' asked Christos.

'Follow the road through Tera and out again,' instructed Kaya.

The vehicle drove though the village and stopped opposite the citrus groves. All three of them, led by Kaya, walked through the trees until he found the spot where Mehmet Bay had found the coin and the tree where Kaya had found the metal object.

'I fell from the top of the hill and tumbled down to here. Mehmet Bay found the gold coin where that piece of wood is, and I found the nail by the base of that tree over there. I think the gold coins would be scattered from the peak of the hill all the way down to where we are standing,' explained Kaya.

'Why don't we start from the top of the hill and work our way down?' Suggested Andrea.

'Sounds logical to me,' answered Kaya, while Christos nodded.

Sitting about 10 feet apart at the top of the hill the

threesome started removing the topsoil searching for the coins and gradually worked their way down the hill making sure they replaced the soil. Their search proved fruitless.

'Are you sure this is the right area?' asked Christos.

'I am not sure now,' said Kaya, sounding slightly despondent.

'Are we all happy if we call it a day?' Kaya asked.

'Yes, I am starting to feel tired. What is the plan for tomorrow?' asked Andrea.

'We start digging around the observation tower,' Kaya said as he made his way to the land rover.

Christos drove Kaya home before he and Andrea drove to the vacant house on the outskirts of the village where they were staying for the duration of the excavation.

The next morning a car horn alerted Kaya and picking up his bag he swiftly made his way outside where Christos and Andrea were waiting for him. Arriving at the site they noticed a car parked on the roadside. The morning proved to be frustrating as again nothing was found.

'It seems that most of the original foundation stones of the fort have been removed and the ones we see are the only remnants,' concluded Kaya.

'Maybe the Byzantines or the Arabs removed them to use to build their churches or mosques,' commented Andrea.

'Good point,' responded Kaya.

'If this is the extent of the site, is it worth the Survey Branch sending a team here?' Christos questioned.

'I would say it certainty does not justify a team of three people, one or maybe two at most. Look, Mr Nicolaou is coming tomorrow, and I think we need to have a meeting with him and discuss the site team,' said Kaya.

Suddenly several gun shots penetrated the air!

'Where's that coming from?' shouted Kaya.

All three of them ran towards the land rover.

'Over there!' yelled Andrea as they saw three men all dressed in black run to the parked car.

One of the men turned around and it became apparent he was carrying a firearm of some sort. The gunman stopped and looked at the three archaeologists, raised his gun and fired into the air Kaya and Christos dived to the ground but Andrea froze, staring at the gunman. The three gunmen hastily got into the car and drove off. Andrea hurried into the road and pointed. A few hundred yards down the road was a British army humber truck. Kaya and Christos joined Andrea and they ran towards the army truck. A tree log lay in front of the truck, and laying beside it were two British soldiers. Kaya attended to one of them careful not to step in the pool of blood.

'I think he is dead,' announced Kaya.

'This one is alive,' Andrea said kneeling over the other soldier.

'We need to drive to the village and get some help,' said Kaya.

'We cannot, the log and truck are blocking the road,' Christos said.

'I will run there,' Kaya said as he started to run down the road.

Before long a police car arrived, Sergeant Yilmaz Constable Ferdi, Dr Aziz and Kaya rushed out of the car to attend to the stricken soldiers. Yilmaz approached Andrea and Christos.

'Did you get a good look at the gunmen?' Questioned Yilmaz.

'No, they were too far way,' Christos said abruptly.

Yilmaz turned to Andrea.

'Would you recognize any of them if you saw them again?'

Andrea shook her head. A couple of army military ambulance arrived followed by a couple of army trucks. Yilmaz walked towards the officer in charge.

'Hello, I am Captain Herrold.'

'Sergeant Yilmaz,' he said shaking the captain's hand.

'EOKA ambush,' Yilmaz clearly stated.

'Did anyone see it?' asked the Captain.

'Yes, three archaeologists heard the shots and said there were three gunmen.'

'Did any of them get a close look of the gunmen? Would they recognize them,' asked the Captain.

'I would.'

Yilmaz turned and Kaya was standing there.

'Could you?' Yilmaz asked.

'Yes, I got a good look of one of the gunman,' re-iterated Kaya.

'How come your two colleagues say they would not be able to identify the gunman if they were the same distance away from them as you,' questioned the Captain.

Kaya shrugged his shoulders.

'It is obvious why,' Yilmaz muttered under his breath.

'Did anyone see the car registration number?' The Capatin asked.

'No sir,' replied Kaya.

The military Doctor approached them, and they could see blankets were covering both soldiers.

'Sorry gentlemen, I'm afraid both soldiers are dead.'

The Captain marched over to view the bodies.

'How well do you know these two?' Yilmaz asked Kaya whist looking at Andrea and Christos.

'I don't really know them. They work for the Archaeological Survey Branch and have been assigned to assist me on the dig.'
'You better head off home,' Yilmaz advised him.

Kaya was reading 'The Decline and Fall of the Roman Empire by Edward Gibbon' outside on the veranda when his father came home.
'What happened? Are you alright?' a concerned Ali asked.
'I am fine, Dad.'
'Sergeant Yilmaz told me there were three of them, and you got a good look at one of them.'
'I did,' confirmed Kaya.
'Did he get a good look at you?'
'Not really, Christos and I dived to the ground, but Andrea just stood there staring at him.'
'I am certain these three are part of the same unit as the men who killed your uncle. Don't worry, their day will come,' Ali ominously said.

Moods were slightly subdued the next day as Nicolaou arrived at the site. 'Murdered' was the headline on the front page of the Cyprus Mail with a photograph from the scene.
'It seems like you all had a very eventful day,' Nicolaou said showing Kaya the paper before pointing out to a sentence in the second paragraph.
'Archaeologists from a nearby excavation site discovered the soldiers,' he read out. 'How do you feel today?' Nicolaou asked.
'I still feel a bit numb,' answered Andrea.
'I think we all do,' said Kaya.
'I have spoken to Mr Megaw and Mr Catling and they have said if you want to, we can stop the excavation. Your

collective decision,' Nicolaou informed them.

Andrea and Christos looked at Kaya for guidance.

'Mr Nicolaou, we had a conversation before yesterday's events unfolded and I, well all three of us believe the site does not require a team of three. I would recommend that me and one other could stay for another few weeks and if nothing of substance is found we close the site,' commented Kaya.

Nicolaou nodded.

'I would be happy to accept your suggestion. Then the question for Andrea and Christos is which one of you would like to stay and assist Kaya?'

Andrea raised her hand.

'I would like to stay,' she said.

'Christos, do you have any objections?' Nicolaou asked him.

'No, I agree with the decision,' Christos said.

'Let us think about the logistics. Christos you can come back with me, and Kaya and Andrea can take the land rover,' Nicolaou suggested.

'Andrea, if you want you can come and stay with my family. We have a spare bedroom, and it would make travel to and from the site easier,' said Kaya.

'That is a good idea, if your family do not mind?' Andrea said.

'No, they won't mind.'

THREE

Scorpions danced to the light of sunrise before scurrying for shelter under the ancient Roman stones. Andrea stood in the freshly dug trench and stretched her arms up to the sky. This act drew Kaya's attention and for a minute archaeology was the last thing on his mind. His gaze caught Andrea's eye and as she turned and smiled at him, he quickly looked down in embarrassment shifting soil with his hands.

'I think I have something,' said Kaya.

Andrea rushed over.

'What is it?'

Kaya brushed away the soil and held out the object to Andrea to take and inspect.

'I think it may be a fragment of some pottery. Maybe a jug or something similar,' she said handing it back to Kaya who threw it into a metal container.

'You are still thinking about the gold coins?'

'Yes, I am still convinced they are somewhere. The Romans would not have described something on a plaque if it was not of any significance. Don't you agree?' He asked Andrea.

'I agree, but we are talking about items buried over eighteen hundred years ago. Any of the Roman soldiers around at the time could have searched for them and maybe found them. Why don't we go there later this afternoon?'

'Yes, we can spend a couple more hours there and if we find nothing then we can forget about it.' agreed Kaya.

A couple more fragments of pottery were found, but nothing to give Kaya or Andrea an adrenaline rush.

'Do you miss Christos?' asked Kaya catching Andrea off-guard.

'I am going to see him at the weekend,' she replied.

'You have been together for a few years. Any sound of wedding bells in the near future?'

'No wedding bells yet,' Andrea said feeling uncomfortable by his questions.

'Sorry Andrea, I do not mean to pry. Please ignore me,' he said looking down into the ground.

Andrea sat closer to him.

'I mean Christos is a handsome man, but I can not see myself marrying him.'

'I am sorry for asking you such personal questions, I think being an archaeologist makes you naturally curious,' said Kaya.

'Do you mean it makes you nosy?'

'Yes!' confirmed Kaya.

Shadows cast by the orange and lemon trees cooled down Kaya and Andrea during their quest to find the gold coins. The ground was baked hard so digging the topsoil was tough going, but once removed they were able to reach the softer earth below. Again, over two hours of digging proved futile. The pair washed their hands and faces in the stream. Kaya took off his boots and socks before rolling up his trousers and wading in.

'Come in,' he urged Andrea.

Andrea was happy to sit on the edge with her feet in the water. Kaya walked up to her before splashing her.

'Stop it!' she shouted.

She stood up wiping her face. Kaya went over and as he

attempted to climb out of the stream Andrea pushed him with both hands and he fell backwards into the water. She pointed and laughed at him. He suddenly jumped out and grabbed her before throwing her into the stream.

'You bastard!' she shouted out.

'Who's laughing now?' Kaya shouted back.

The soaked pair made their way through the fields.

'Have you two been swimming?' A voice from behind them asked, startling them.

Mehmet Bay stood behind them.

'We were in the stream,' said Kaya.

'Come to my house to dry off,' offered Mehmet Bay as he surged ahead of them and led them to his house.

'Fahriye, we have guests,' shouted Mehmet Bay.

Fahriye, his wife, came out and instantly recognised Kaya.

'My goodness you are both wet. Let me bring you some towels to dry yourselves,' she said rushing back into the house.

'Have you found anything interesting on your dig?' Mehmet Bay asked.

'No, nothing of great interest,' replied Kaya.

'You have not found any Roman coins?'

Kaya shook his head as Fahriye came back and handed a towel to Kaya and Andrea, and a dress to Andrea and shirt and trousers to Kaya.

'What is this about Roman coins?' asked a curious Fahriye.

'We found an inscription on a plaque at the Roman fort describing a tribute of Roman coins that probably lay on the hill side of Mehmet Bay's land, where the orange and lemon trees are,' explained Kaya.

'Did he show the coin he found years ago?'

'I did,' intervened Mehmet Bay.

'Go and get changed out of the wet clothes,' Fahriye urged them. 'The girl can go into the bedroom on the left and you can go into the room to the right,' she told Kaya.

Kaya and Andrea came out and Fahriye grabbed the wet clothes from them and hanged them onto the washing line. The outside table was set with plates and cutlery.

'Sit down,' said Fahriye hurrying back inside.

Andrea felt a bit awkward as she looked at Kaya and he beckoned her to sit down. Fahriye came out carrying a large bowl of cut watermelon and placed in the middle of the table.

'Go on help yourselves,' said Mehmet Bay.

Fahriye sat next to Andrea.

'Where is your family from?'

'A village near Paralimni,' answered Andrea.

'So, you have not found the gold Roman coins?'

'Well, we do not know for sure if there are any coins, we are just going by the inscription we found at the fort ruins,' commented Kaya.

'My Dede used to tell me that there was a story that a trove of Roman coins was buried somewhere in the Village. All the land on both sides of the stream was owned by my great-great grandfather, Abdullah Cavus, and maybe he found the Roman coins and buried it somewhere,' Fahriye told Kaya and Andrea.

'Was your Dede Haji Hodja?' asked Kaya.

'His name was Osman Nuri, and he was a schoolteacher and Imam of the village and in 1902 he travelled all the way to Mecca on a Haj. That's why everyone knew him as Haji Hodja,' explained Fahriye.

'And did he build the water fountains in the village?' Asked Kaya.

'Yes, he helped raise the money to build it. The pipe had originally been built by the Venetians and Abdullah Cavus found it when he first arrived at the village. Anyway, you two must stay for dinner,' said Fahriye.

'No, my mum is expecting us back.'

'No, your mum will understand. We cannot have guests and not invite them to stay for dinner,' she insisted.

Mehmet Bay shrugged his shoulders. Fahriye had prepared etli bezelye, lamb and pea casserole. Kaya and Andrea were obliged to stay.

After changing back into their own clothes, they thanked Mehmet Bay and Fahriye for their hospitality and made they way home.

'Where are you going?' asked Andrea as Kaya walked down the road heading towards the water fountains.

'I want to show you the fountain.'

The water fountain had two tiers, the top tier had three large arches and the bottom tier had five smaller arches, each with water pouring out of a central pipe. The inscription on the top said Terra House and in the middle of the fountain had 1904 inscribed on a plaque.

'I really like this village,' Andrea said.

'Tera is great, but I don't see my future here. I mean not even in Cyprus. There are so many places I want to travel to and live in. It will always be my home, but for my career to progress I need to move away,' Kaya confided to her.

'I know how you feel Kaya. I studied abroad and you do not know how difficult that is for a woman. My intention was exactly like yours, come back here, work for a few years gaining experience to then apply for a university abroad.'

'Have you changed your mind?' he asked.

'It is so difficult for a woman; family pressure is so enormous. Pleasing my parents is the most important thing in the World for me and I do not want to disappoint them.'

'But, how exactly have you disappointed them, you are intelligent, have a dream job. Where is the disappointment?'

'All my parents want is for me is to settle down, get married and have a family,' explained Andrea.

'Yes, but that's a generation thing. My Father didn't want me to study abroad and certainly was against me studying archaeology. In the end he came round and realised that my happiness was the most important thing. Maybe your parents need to understand about what you want and what makes you happy now and in the future.'

'Maybe,' said Andrea as she held Kaya's hand.

They walked past the village café and the men sat outside all stared at the pair.

'Kaya is that your Greek girlfriend?' Shouted one of the men.

'Are you having sex with her?' Shouted another which led to rapturous of laughter from the other men.

'Get lost!' Kaya shouted back as he held Andrea's hand tighter.

A couple of men got up from the chairs and began to follow them.

'Just carry-on walking,' Kaya told Andrea.

'Kaya!' shouted one of the men.

'Hey, college boy we want to talk to you,' shouted the other man.

Kaya stopped and turned around. It was too dark to make them out but as he walked towards them, he recognised them as Ferdi and Murat.

'Why don't you two just go home?' Kaya told them.

'We just want to ask you what it's like screwing a Greek girl?' said Ferdi as he nudged Murat, and both started laughing.

Kaya started advancing towards them, but Andrea pulled him back.

'Come on, ignore them, let's go,' Andrea urged him.

Kaya turned and with Andrea, started walking again. Ferdi ran up towards them.

'I heard all Greek girls are very friendly. Are you very friendly?' Ferdi asked grabbing the top of Andrea's blouse.

Kaya pushed Ferdi's arm away and pushed him so hard Ferdi stumbled backwards into bushes by the side of the road. Murat ran up and swung a punch at Kaya who blocked it with his left arm and punched him with his right hand knocking him to the ground. Ferdi picked up a large stone from the side of the road and threatened Kaya.

'Come on college boy!'

At this point bright headlights blinded Kaya and Andrea and the roar of a motorcycle made them step back in fright. The bike came to an abrupt stop. Off the bike climbed a policeman, it was Sergeant Yilmaz.

'Have I missed the party?' commented Yilmaz.

'Ask him Sergeant,' said Kaya pointing at Ferdi.

'Ferdi, put that stone down.'

Ferdi dropped the stone onto the ground as Murat managed to get up blood visible on his face.

Yilmaz walked up to Andrea.

'Were these two bothering you?'

'Yes,' she answered.

Yilmaz went up to Ferdi and Murat.

'If you don't start walking home in the next ten seconds I will arrest the pair of you,' stated Yilmaz in a loud, stern voice.

Without hesitation the pair turned and briskly walked off. Yilmaz got back on his bike.

'You two get home as well,' he said to Kaya and Andrea.

'Thank you, Sergeant!' Andrea said loudly as Yilmaz went past.

'Sergeant Yilmaz was the policeman who shot the EOKA gunman who killed my uncle,' Kaya informed her.

'So, he killed Michalis?'

'Yes,' replied Kaya.

A few minutes later they reached Kaya's house. His parents were asleep, so they decided to sit outside on the veranda. Kaya disappeared into the house and a few minutes later re-emerged holding a bottle of brandy and two glasses. Andrea laughed when she saw him.

'Is that what your dad drinks?' She asked.

'Don't tell me your dad drinks this as well?'

'That is the only thing he drinks,' confirmed Andrea.

Kaya poured the brandy and sat next to her.

'You were quite a hero tonight,' said Andrea.

'What do you mean?'

'How you stood up to those two drunks.'

'Those two are both idiots. I've been fighting them since I was five years old.' Kaya told her.

'This actually tastes quite nice,' Andrea said sipping the brandy.

She rested her head on Kaya's shoulder and he turned to be face to face with her. Staring into each other's eyes they kissed. Andrea finished off her brandy in one gulp. Kaya was impressed by this and did the same before pouring more brandy. A full moon lit their faces and Kaya blew out the outside oil lamp, they kissed and cuddled to the sound of the crickets.

A loud noise from outside woke Kaya up, he rubbed the sleep from his eyes and accidently nudged Andrea, who was lying next to him, waking her up. Kaya jumped out of bed to look out of the window and realised he was totally naked.

'Oh!' he muttered.

'I better get to my room,' said Andrea slowly climbing out of bed to reveal her nakedness.

'Ooops,' she said in an embarrassed tone.

Kaya raised his eyebrows and threw her a towel. After wrapping the towel around her, she peered out the door to see if the coast was clear and turned to Kaya.

'I'll see you for breakfast,' she said dashing across the corridor to her room.

The awkwardness at the table was only too apparent as Nalan served breakfast.

'You two are quiet. What time did you get back?' asked Nalan.

Kaya and Andrea stared at each other and smiled.

'I don't think it was that late,' replied Kaya.

Nalan surprised them by showing the empty brandy bottle.

'I was going to tell Dad about that. Andrea and I had a couple of nightcaps.'

'A couple,' Nalan said sarcastically.

'I'll buy dad another bottle later.'

At that moment Ali walked in and Nalan swiftly hid the bottle under her blouse.

'I have to go to Kritou, if you want, I can give you a lift to the ruins, saves you driving there.' Ali offered.

'Thanks Dad, but we are going to drive to Polis now before going to the site.'

Ali left and Nalan wrapped the bottle in some newspaper and placed it in the bin.

Andrea placed her hand on Kaya's thigh as he drove to the site, he reciprocated by taking his left hand off the steering wheel and placing it on her thigh. They both leaned to each other and kissed.

'If those drunken idiots ever ask you again, what is it like to screw a Greek girl, you can tell them.'

Kaya smiled at her comment.

'Christos is not going to be happy if he ever finds out,' he said.

'I think what last night proved is that me and Christos are no longer together.'

'When are you going to tell him that?'

'Yes, that is going to be the difficult part, but don't worry I am not going to mention us, or it will cause to much stress on our working relationship,' she explained.

Reaching the site, Kaya parked the car in the shade under a tree and looked at his watch.

'We're early. What should we do now?' he asked as he started to undo the buttons on Andrea's blouse which prompted her to start undoing his trousers. A few moments later they clambered into the back seat. Some ten minutes later Kaya stumbled out of the vehicle.

'We better start doing some work,' he shouted out.

Kaya had dug the area around the plaque and unearthed a stone that had symbols carved on it.

'Andrea, come here.'

'What have you found?'

He brushed away the earth, so the symbols became clearer.

'Exercitus castrium,' he shouted out.

'What does that mean?' Andrea asked.

'Army camp.' Kaya shouted.

Andrea knelt for closer inspection.

'By the looks of it, it may well have been at the entrance of the camp,' he said prizing the stone from the ground before lifting onto a set of other stones.

'I saw these symbols the other night,' Andrea recalled.

'Where?'

'At the water fountains in Tera.'

'Where at the water fountains?'

'Under one of the water pipes. I thought someone must have carved the symbols onto the fountain,' she explained.

'The fountain was built in 1904 so how would anyone have known the meaning of those symbols?' We may have to ask Mehmet Bay and his wife some more questions,' he added.

'Do you think Sergeant Yilmaz would know some of the history of the village?' asked Andrea.

'He may well do, but I don't know what days he comes to the village now that he is living in Polis and I think he has more important things occupying him.'

'How did he manage to track down Michalis?'

'My uncle was at the café and Michalis and his accomplice rode up on a motorbike and shot him. Luckily one of the villagers saw and remembered the registration number of the bike. Yilmaz and his unit found the bike and waited for Michalis and the other gunman and ambushed them. My dad thinks the gunmen who killed the British Soldiers are part of the same EOKA cell operating in this area. What are your views?'

'My views on what?'

'EOKA, Enosis, the British, the future of Cyprus,' said Kaya.

'I have very strong views,' she said.

A moment or two passed.

'Are you going to share them with me?' asked Kaya.

'My view is that Cyprus belongs to the Cypriots and not the British. The sooner they leave and give us independence the better.'

'Do you then believe that the terrorists are justified in killing British soldiers and policeman?'

Andrea was silent.

'Were they justified in murdering my uncle?' he asked.

Andrea felt uneasy by Kaya's line of questioning and realizing this he stood up and looked at his watch.

'Shall we go to Polis?' he asked.

'You don't have to change the subject,' she said.

'I could sense that you did not feel comfortable talking about it. So, don't feel obliged if you do not want to,' replied Kaya.

'One death because of the troubles is one death too many, but the ends must justify the means. Unfortunately, the only way we can liberate ourselves is to fight for our freedom. Many people have died Greek Cypriot, Turkish Cypriot, and British people and many more will die until we achieve our independence. The island should be governed by Cypriots for the Cypriots, both Greek and Turkish,' she said passionately.

'I agree with you that Cyprus should be governed by all Cypriots, but vehemently disagree with those Greeks who support Enosis. They want Cyprus to be part of Greece, one big Hellenic Republic, but what happens to Turkish Cypriots? What happens to me? What happens to my family?' questioned Kaya.

'I am against Enosis, all it will mean is the Island being ruled by Greece rather than the British,' she said.

'But that solution would be appealing to quite a lot of Greek Cypriots. Same language, same religion, same culture. What is there not to like?' He asked.

'Many members of my family support it, but I personally do not.'

Polis was a provincial town located at the heart of Chrysochou Bay and closest town to Tera. Kaya drove into the car park located between the church and the main square.

'The post office is on the other side of the main square,' said Kaya said vaguely pointing in that direction.

'I have some letters to post,' replied Andrea.

'Once I have bought the brandy I'll come and meet you there.'

'No, I will meet you back here in an hour,' she said firmly. Kaya looked at his watch.

'It is eleven o'clock now, so meet you back here by midday.'

Andrea kissed him on the cheek and briskly walked off holding her bag tightly. That put a big smile on Kaya's face. People were rushing to do what they needed to before the midday sun caught them. Kaya somehow enjoyed this hustle and bustle of the town, weaving in and out of people on the narrow pavements. The main square was always a hive of activity and the presence of British soldiers compounded it. Arsinoe Stores was probably named after the ancient name for Polis, the old harbour used by the Romans. Kaya entered the store to be met by row upon row of wine and spirit bottles. It took a while for him to locate the bottle he was looking for, Five Kings Brandy. He queued up behind a couple of Soldiers who were holding four bottles of beer each.

'Where in England are you from?' asked Kaya engaging in polite conversation. One of soldiers turned to him and gave him a look of disdain.

'We are not from England,' said the solider in a heavy

Irish accent.

'Oh sorry,' said Kaya as he took a step back.

'We are from Belfast in Northern Ireland, here with the Royal Ulster Rifles,' confirmed the much friendly second soldier.

'I am sorry. I should have asked what part of Britain you are from.'

'Your English is pretty good,' the second soldier said.

'I went to the English school in Nicosia and spent three years at University in England.'

'We've been in Cyprus for about three months, this is our first overseas tour.'

'How are you finding the Island?' Kaya asked.

'Far too hot for us, but I love swimming in the sea,' said the soldier as he approached the counter with his compatriot to pay for the beers.

'A cold beer come in handy on a hot day,' Kaya commented.

'Yes, we're going to take them back to the camp once we finish our patrol today. We have a bucket of cold water in the back of the truck to keep them cool. Anyway, have a good day,' the soldier said to Kaya as the pair left the shop.

Kaya paid for the brandy and made his way back to the car park. He carefully wrapped the bottle in a cloth before placing it a compartment in the boot of the car. The time was 11.30am so he still had half an hour to kill before Andrea came back, so he decided to have a wander around the town. Feeling particularly peckish, the smell of freshly baked bread drew him towards a small bakery opposite the car park. Aphrodite Bakery not only sold bread but freshly made sandwiches.

'Can I help you?' asked the lady standing behind the

counter.

'Yes, can I have a halloumi and tomatoes in the corek seeded bread.'

The lady sliced the bread in a flash spread a scoop of butter on it before adding a layer of halloumi and a layer of large, sliced tomatoes on top. She wrapped it in paper and handed to Kaya who handed over the money. Benches surrounded the main square and Kaya was lucky enough to find an empty bench to sit and devour his sandwich. Juice from the tomatoes dripped onto his shirt and he took out a handkerchief from his pocket and tried to wipe the stain off but inadvertently spread the stain making it look worse. As lunchtime approached footfall increased and he watched as two old ladies meandered around the square searching for a vacant bench. Kaya spotted them and beckoned them over. The Ladies thanked him, and he decided to make his way to the post office to see if he could find Andrea.

Walking towards the post office his gaze was drawn to a man who had just come out of the post office. Recognising the man, his memory took a few seconds to calculate who he was. Kaya stopped. It was one of the gunmen that had shot the British soldiers near the Roman site. The man was wearing black shirt and black trousers, and after a few yards he stopped and looked back in the direction of the post office. Kaya was unable to fathom out what to do. At that point two soldiers walked past Kaya and in that spilt second, he decided to go and tell them that he recognized a EOKA gunman.

'Excuse me!' Kaya shouted out.

But the soldiers did not hear him. Kaya then quickly followed them.

'Excuse me, Soldiers!'

The soldiers stopped and turned round. They were the two Irish soldiers from the shop who bought the beers. Kaya pointed into the direction of the post office, suddenly he saw Andrea come out the post office and gesticulate to the gunman who nodded back at her.

'How are you doing?' One of soldiers asked Kaya.

Kaya was distracted watching Andrea.

'Can we help you?' asked the soldier.

'No, I just wanted to say to enjoy the beers,' he replied.

The soldiers stared at him as he walked past them and towards Andrea. The gunman had disappeared, and Andrea smiled as she noticed Kaya walking towards her. He was perplexed by the situation and managed to force a smile out as he reached Andrea.

FOUR

Kaya was at a loss. Did he just imagine the scenario from the previous day? Did he really see Andrea, the girl he wanted to spend every waking minute with, and an EOKA gunman together? Maybe the midday sun had distorted his memory and the man outside the post office was not the man who murdered the two British soldiers? Too many questions for his mind to cope with this early in the day, distracting from what he should be focusing on, the dig at the Roman site. Andrea had left to visit her parents for a few days giving him a period of reflection, but this was not the type of reflection he wanted.

'What are your plans for today,' his father asked him.

'I'm going to the site.'

'But it is the weekend, are you not entitled to two days off?'

'Yes, but I would rather carry-on working,' said Kaya.

The journey to the site became a fuzzy haze due to Andrea preoccupying his mind, and this led down the natural path to his heart. Pouring water over his head from his bottle seemed to wake him from Andrea's spell. He found the stone that had the inscription symbols 'Exercitus Castrum' and this made him remember Andrea's comment that she had seen the very same symbols at the water fountain in Tera. This made him wonder why these symbols would be on a feature that was erected in the early nineteenth century? This question made him put down his trowel and drive back to Tera. Villagers were filling up canisters of water from the fountain, for some this was their only source of fresh water.

'Kaya!'

A sharp voice startled him.

'Kaya, how are you?'

He turned to see a middle-aged woman dressed head to toe in black and it took him a few seconds to work out who it was.

'Belge Hanim, I am well. How are you? It has been a long time since I last saw you,'

'Have you found any treasure yet?' she said laughing at the same time with two other women who stood next to her.

'Not yet Belge Hanim.'

'Are you coming to Ferdi's wedding? The henna ceremony is tomorrow at our house.'

Kaya hesitated for a moment. He did overhear his parents talking about the wedding but was not really on his list of priorities right now.

'I bumped into Ferdi the other night,' he said.

'He didn't say anything to me,' she said with surprise.

'It was a brief meeting,' he said unwilling to expand on the circumstances of his encounter with Ferdi any further.

'If you cannot make the ceremony tomorrow you must come to the reception on Sunday. You are one of his oldest friends,' Belge Hanim said totally oblivious to Kaya and her son's true relationship. One that you couldn't really describe as friendship.

'I wouldn't miss it for the World. Who is the lucky lady?

'A girl from Arodes. She comes from a very good family, and she is very beautiful,' she boasted.

'Yes, I will be there,' he confirmed before the ladies said goodbye and left.

Clear of people, Kaya wandered over to the fountain and

closely examined the arches. And there they were, the Latin symbols that spelt out "army camp" inscribed below the pipe of the middle arch. Further down on a stone panel below the trough where the water flowed, he noticed another faint inscription. Carefully brushing away the dirt and dust he recognised the writing was Arabic. As he was unable to read Arabic, he took out his note pad and copied the writing hoping he could translate it when he got home.

Village weddings were usually a three-day affair. It was Thursday and in Arodes Ferdi's bride to be, Zehra, was preparing to have her hands covered in henna. The powdered form of henna comes from the plant known as Lawsonia inermis and is made into paste before being applied on the skin. Zehra first put on her white dress, before she laid the palms of her hands down on the table. Zehra's aunt firstly cleaned Zehra's hands and arms with warm water that had been heated over the fire stove. The henna was then applied to the palms of Zehra's hands, before an old lady uttered blessings in Arabic. Zehra's mother came into the bedroom and kissed her daughter, and a few seconds later a blast of sound came from outside. Zehra opened the window to see two men playing the duval and zurna. The duval is a drum that is held by the drummer at waist level by a strap. The zurna is a double-reed woodwind instrument. It is loud and strident, so suitable to being played outdoors. Both the players were dressed in bright red shirts, and gold waistcoats and black trousers, and both men wore red and gold hats. Zehra was escorted out of the house by her mother and aunt, and waiting outside was her father who was holding a donkey. He assisted Zehra to mount the animal before the men playing the duval and zurna walked in front of the donkey and led the procession through the village.

Villagers joined the end of the procession as it wound its way around the streets of Arodes. Simultaneously the same act was being performed in Tera. Ferdi was dressed to the nines in a pure white shirt with gold cufflinks and white trousers complemented by brown shoes and belt. Henna was placed on the palms of his hands by his grandmother and as she kissed him on both cheeks, the duval and zurna burst into sound. A horse stood outside waiting for Ferdi, and the drummer paced up and down to the rhythm of the duval's beat. Ferdi mounted the horse and just like the procession in Arodes began to work its way through Tera. The duval and zurna acting as a pied piper leading the villagers out of their homes to join the extending procession. Preparation of the wedding food was in full swing. A cauldron of harees was being stirred again and again, teenagers taking turns to mix the ingredients with a large wooden ladle. Harees, also known as keskek was made from cracked wheat laid over boneless lamb meat. Boiling water was then poured over the mixture before the task of stirring the ingredients together. The meat would melt until it became like a form of porridge. Another staple dish at wedding was kolokas, chicken and taro root stew, made from twenty large chickens. Tables and chairs were being set up in the village school yard, not only did they need to cater for the inhabitants of Tera but also all guests arriving from the brides' village. All in all, over 200 people were expected to be in attendance. Ferdi's parents stood at the entrance to the school welcoming guests as they arrived. A few minutes later the parents of Zehra arrived and stood next to Ferdi's parents. Guests started arriving, first a trickle which rapidly became a steady flow including the guests from Arodes.

The Mustafa family arrived, Kaya walking behind his parents and brother and sister.
'Ali, your family can sit on the second table at the front,' Ferdi's mum said grabbing the sleeve of Ali's shirt.
Humidity was making it an uncomfortable night for all in attendance. Most men were wearing shirts and trousers and the women summer dresses. The incessant noise of the guests gradually fell silent upon hearing the distant sound of the duval and zurna hastening the arrival of the bride and groom. Kaya sat down with his family and sitting on the next table was Sergeant Yilmaz and his family, Kaya found it strange seeing Yilmaz without his uniform on and the pair acknowledged each other, as the men playing the duval and zurna entered the area closely followed by Ferdi and his new bride. Zehra looked beautiful in her wedding dress, the whiteness of the dress enhancing her tanned face and her olive green eyes. Ferdi also looked resplendent in his all white suit and brown floral design tie. The players led the bride and groom in a circle around the center of the tables. Kaya's thoughts were still with Andrea and the EOKA gunman, and in his mind, he found it difficult to separate the two. He glanced across to the other table to see Yilmaz's face, before he turned his gaze to his deceased Uncle's wife and three young children. His head was pounding urging him to say something to Yilmaz, but his heart was beating even louder telling him it was all a coincidence and wanting to be with Andrea.

The next night Kaya lit the oil lamp in his bedroom, electricity had yet to reach this part of Cyprus, which frustrated Kaya but he knew plans were in place to bring it to Tera and surrounding villages thus steering them into the modern era. Translating from Arabic was far more arduous than translating from Latin. He couldn't be one hundred percent certain that what he copied from the inscription on the water fountain was correct, but what he had translated came as a revelation. Roughly it translated into: -

Hadrian, Emperor of Rome dedicated this tribute to the legatoro of Cyprus...now this tribute is dedicated to the village of Tera for its future prosperity.

Kaya read the translation three or four times but still could not fathom the meaning. Maybe he was mis-translating some of the words. In his mind he kept repeating the same question, are the gold Roman coins buried under the water fountain? He rushed out of the house as quietly as possible, as his mother and siblings were asleep, his father had gone to the café, picking up his bag of tools on the way and putting it in the back of his dad's truck. He went into the outhouse and re-emerged moments later with a pickaxe and a small bag of cement and loaded them into the truck. Speckled lights from the houses dotted Kaya's journey to the fountain. He parked the truck nearby and turned the lights off as he could see some people hanging around the fountain. Kaya wound down the truck window allowing in the constant chatter of the men outside the café. The sound of a motorbike engine crept up and as he looked in his rear view mirror the beam of the bikes' lights made him turn his head away. The bike roared past him before coming to a sudden halt outside the café. Kaya took out the binoculars from its case and was able to recognize that the rider was Sergeant Yilmaz.

Some of the men greeted him and he sat down at one of the outside tables. A few minutes later a car drove past the truck at a pedestrian pace.

'Shit!' Kaya blurted out.

He turned on the truck headlight at full beam. It was the same car used by the gunmen to shoot the British Soldiers. Kaya switched off the lights, turned on the ignition, and began to follow the car. The car stopped outside the café with its engine still on, Kaya stopped the truck fifty or so yards behind them. The front passenger car door opened, and a man dressed all in black got out. Kaya turned on the truck lights and this made the man turn towards the truck, Kaya saw that the man was holding a gun in his right hand. Kaya put his foot down on the accelerator and sounded the car horn alerting the men sat outside the café, most of whom ran inside. The truck slammed into the back of the car and the impact made the gunman fall to the ground and his left leg somehow got caught under the car and he let out an audible groan.

'EOKA?' shouted Kaya through the car window.

Yilmaz turned a table on its side, drew his pistol and started shooting at the car. Two men came running out of the café each carrying a rifle and they both knelt on the ground before shooting at the car, one of them was Ali, Kaya's father. The driver of the car pulled the gunman into the car and drove off, the rear bumper guard hanging off the car. Yilmaz, Ali, and the other man ran onto the road and continued shooting at the car as it vanished into the night. Kaya got out of the truck and Ali rushed over to him.

'Are you hurt?' a concerned Ali asked Kaya.

'I am fine. I was more worried about you.'

'As you can see, we were prepared for them,' Ali said

showing off his rifle. 'What are you doing driving my truck?'

'I drove to the fountain to look for something,' said Kaya trying not to give too much information away.

Yilmaz walked over and put his arm around Kaya.

'Thank you, you have probably just saved my life,' he told Kaya.

'I recognized the car; it was the same car the gunman used to kill the soldiers. I was parked near the fountain, and I saw you arrive on your motorbike and their car followed soon after. Obviously, they were after you,' concluded Kaya.

'Did you get a view of the gunman?' asked Yilmaz.

'Yes, it was definitely the same gunman who shot the soldiers.'

Kaya was on the verge of telling Yilmaz that he had seen the same gunman in Polis seemingly knowing Andrea, but he bit his lip.

'I need to go to Kritou and telephone the camp,' Yilmaz said annoyed at the fact that there was no telephone line in Tera.

'Sergeant, I must tell you something, something important. I saw the same gunman in Polis a couple of days ago. He came out of the post office,' Kaya blurted out.

'Thanks for letting me know. Can you come to police station in Polis tomorrow. We have photographs of suspected EOKA members. Maybe you can recognize the gunman from the photos,' Yilmaz said as he got onto his bike.

'Are you going by bike?' Ali asked.

'I'm not going to walk,' Yilmaz responded.

'For all you know they could be laying in wait for you. Leave your bike here and I'll take you in the truck,' insisted Ali.

'You're right,' said Yilmaz.

Yilmaz wheeled his motorbike by the side of the café and he Ali and Kaya got into the truck. Just outside Tera Ali slowed down as he could see a car parked on the side of the road; it was the gunmen's car.

'Park behind it,' ordered Yilmaz as he loaded his pistol with bullets.

Ali parked the truck behind the car and picked up his rifle that was next to him.

'Kaya you stay in the truck,' Yilmaz told him,

Ali and Yilmaz got out of the truck and tentatively walked towards the car. Yilmaz knelt looking into the car through the back window, the glass was riddled with bullet holes and both back tyres were flat.

'They've abandoned the car,' proclaimed Yilmaz.

Ali pointed his rifle towards the fields as Yilmaz opened the driver's car door and shined his torch. Blood was evident on the passenger's seat.

'We may have shot one of the gunmen. Let's continue to Kritou. There are probably out in the field,' Yilmaz said.

Ali and Yilmaz got back into the truck and drove off.

'Dad, where did you get the rifle from?

Yilmaz gave a side glance towards Ali.

'It has come to a point that us Turks must arm ourselves. EOKA are not just targeting British Soldiers, but the Turkish Cypriot police. These hardline Greeks not only want independence but Enosis, they want to unify with Greece to form a Hellenic Republic,' explained Ali.

'I know all that Dad, but where have you got the guns from?'

Yilmaz looked straight ahead and kept silent.

'We have a number of friends who are helping us. Many Turkish units have been formed and many more will be formed in every village. We will not stand idly by and let the Greeks take over the Island. We are not second-class citizens on this Island and if necessary, we will fight so we have the same equality as the Greeks,' explained Ali.

'Kaya, are you certain the gunman you saw tonight was the same man you saw in Polis the other day?' asked Yilmaz again.

'Yes, I am certain.'

'You said you saw him coming out of the post office?'

'That is right,' confirmed Kaya.

'What were you doing there?'

'I was buying something for my dad.'

'At the post office?' questioned Yilmaz.

Kaya felt uncomfortable at Yilmaz's line of questioning and was making him sweat profusely. He still wasn't sure whether to mention Andrea, as even though he had questioned it in his mind a thousand times he still wasn't one hundred per cent convinced if she had any involvement with the gunman.

'No, I was walking past the post office when I saw him come out,' Kaya said vehemently.

An hour or so later soldiers from the Royal Ulster Rifles had arrived just outside Tera. Roadblocks were set up between Tera and Polis and soldiers started searching the fields near the abandoned car. Ali and Kaya arrived home.

'I want to go to Lefkosa tomorrow. I'm trying to translate an Arabic inscription that is on the village fountain, but there are some words I cannot understand. Dr Aziz from the museum is an expert in Arabic history so I am hoping he can help me with the translation,' Kaya told Ali.

Kaya then went to his room and collapsed onto his bed physically and emotionally drained by the evening's events.

Two soldiers stood by the gate entrance of the museum car park as Kaya approached the gate in his car. He wound down the window and showed one of the soldiers his pass, who duly opened the gate whilst the other soldier waived Kaya inside. Kaya also wanted to see Mr Catling and give him an update on the excavation, but on his way to Catling's office he ran into Christos in the corridor, and they shook hands.

'How are you?' Christos asked.

'I am very well, Christos.'

'You are both here today,' said Christos.

'What do you mean both here?' questioned Kaya.

'I just saw Andrea in the staff room. She tells me you have found some interesting inscriptions.'

'Yes, that is why I am here. I found an inscription in Arabic, and I want to ask Dr Aziz to translate it. So, how are things with you, are you enjoying the excavation in Paphos?' asked Kaya.

'Wonderful, I found a vase, fully intact dating back over 2,000 years. So many artifacts have been discovered, that we are building a picture of what life was like on the Island during the time of Alexander the Great. Once you have wrapped up the excavation of Tera you will be needed at Paphos. Andrea told me that you have not found anything of great significance,' said Christos.

'She is correct. The only interesting thing has been the inscriptions that keep referencing Roman gold coins. That would be one hell of a discovery,' said Kaya with a glint in his eye.

'That would be amazing. Anyway, I must head off back to Paphos. Look after Andrea for me,' Christos said heading off.

Kaya quickly walked to the staff room but there was no

sign of Andrea, so he wandered along the corridor trying to locate Dr Aziz's office. After climbing a flight of stairs, he turned around and realised that he was well and truly lost. There was not even anybody he could ask so he knocked on the nearest office door he could find, but there was no answer, he tried to open it to find that it was locked, he tried all the office doors, and they were all locked. Deciding to trace his steps back he ran down the flight of stairs and again he was unsure in which direction he came from as all the corridors were identical. The element of comical farce had now been extinguished and descended into embarrassment.

'Are you lost?'

A startled Kaya turned round to see Andrea standing there with a wide smile.

'Andrea,' he said with a sense of relief as they embraced and kissed each other.

'What are you doing here?' Kaya asked her.

'I was going to ask you the same question.'

'I'm here to see Dr Aziz. Below the Roman inscription on the fountain that you found I discovered some faint inscriptions in Arabic. I tried to translate it as best I could but some of the writing, I could not understand, so I want to ask Dr Aziz if could translate it,' explained Kaya.

'I am here to see Mr Catling, his words over the phone were I would like to discuss something with you. Speaking to Christos I think he wants me to transfer to the Paphos excavation.'

They held each other unable to contain the intense feeling the pair had. Passionately kissing each other, it became increasingly difficult to keep their hands off each other.

'God, it feels so good to touch you again,' Kaya said letting out his feelings.

'Me too. I did miss you. It's a shame we are at work today. I would love to spend the whole day and night with you,' said an equally emotional Andrea.

A lady walked out from one of the rooms and the pair backed off.

'Come on, I'll show you Dr Aziz's office,' Andrea said grabbing Kaya by the hand and walking down the corridor.

Andrea stopped outside an office door.

'This is his office,' she said.

'Why don't you come in as well?' he asked.

'Mr Catling is waiting for me. I'll meet you in the staff room afterwards,' she said before planting a kiss on Kaya's lips.

'I want to give him an update, but I'll see Dr Aziz first.'

Kaya knocked on the door.

'Come in,' came the muffled voice from inside the office.

'See you later,' he whispered to Andrea before entering the office.

Dr Aziz hid behind his large desk and oversized circular black framed glasses; his strands of white hair matching his goatee beard and was writing a letter. Kaya stood in front of his desk

'Take a seat young man.'

Kaya sat down while Dr Aziz continued writing.

'Apologies, but I need to write and send off this letter today,' he said.

'Take as long as you like Dr Aziz,' responded Kaya.

Kaya was intrigued by the eclectic range of books in the bookshelf behind Dr Aziz. Apart from the standard history books, some written in Arabic, were a couple of books, on the history of jazz music and many sports books including a pictorial history of the football World Cup from 1930 to

1954 which particularly caught Kaya's eye. By the side of the Doctor's desk was a slender table with a book on it. Kaya squinted his eyes, trying to read the book, only to decipher that it was written in Arabic.

'I see you are interested in the book,' Dr Aziz said pointing at the book on the table.

'I was just wondering why it's on the table,' said Kaya.

'That book is the oldest copy of the Quran on this Island. It is about 450 years old,' confirmed Dr Aziz.

Dr Aziz suddenly stood up.

'Come and see,' he said to Kaya.

Kaya stood and walked towards the doctor, who started to turn the pages of the book.

'This book was printed in the late fifteenth century. It was printed in Istanbul and was probably brought over by the Ottomans when they conquered the Island in 1571. It was originally owned by the Ottoman Governor of the Island, Koca Bekir Pasha, and he was known as a great philanthropist who bequeathed this copy to the Governors Palace,' explained Dr Aziz as he turned the pages of the book trying to be as delicate as possible.

'It is so ornate; it must be priceless?' Kaya uttered.

'Yes, as you can see the elaborate detail is amazing. Very hard to imagine that this is almost five hundred years old,' said Dr Aziz.

Dr Aziz returned behind his desk and sat down. Kaya followed.

'I hear you want me to translate some Arabic inscriptions, come let me see them.' said Dr Aziz.

Kaya took out the various pieces of paper and placed them on the desk in front of Dr Aziz.

'I attempted to translate the Arabic inscription as you can see but I couldn't decipher some of the words,' Kaya told him pointing to the relevant sections of the papers.

Dr Aziz examined the papers. After a few minutes he started writing on a plain sheet of paper. Kaya squinted, his eyes attempting to read the words Dr Aziz was writing. Dr Aziz compared the Arabic inscription with Kaya's translation before comparing it to his translation.

'Mr Mustafa, your translation is very close, but it actually translates:

'Hadrian, Emperor of Rome dedicated this tribute to the legatoro of Cyprus. Now this tribute is dedicated to the village of Tera and the future prosperity of the village lie under the orange trees.'

Kaya took a few moments to digest what he had just heard.

'So, the tribute that is described are the Roman gold coins scatted on the hillside beside Tera that is inscribed on a stone plaque at the Roman fort?' asked Dr Aziz.

'Correct Doctor.'

'Several thoughts cross my mind. Whoever wrote this inscription in Arabic must have seen the Roman plaque. When was the fountains built?' Dr Aziz asked.

'1904. It was built by Haji Hodja, the grandfather of Mehmet Bay who owns the land where the orange trees are,' confirmed Kaya.

'What is interesting is where it states, the future prosperity of the village lies under the orange trees. To me the most interesting question is did Haji Hodja find the tribute?'

'Mehmet Bay showed me the one Roman coin he found years ago, but he says he has never ever found anymore,' Kaya told Dr Aziz.

'Maybe he tells the truth, maybe Haji Hodja was just

making a copy of the Roman inscription or maybe he found the gold coins and buried it elsewhere,' said Dr Aziz.

This certainly provided Kaya with food for thought.

Andrea was sat in the staff room as Kaya burst into the room unable to hide his excitement.

'What are your plans for the rest of the day?' He asked Andrea.

Before she had time to gather her thoughts and give an answer, Kaya grabbed her hand.

'You are coming with me,' he said pulling her up from the chair.

'Where to?' She said has he whisked her around the room.

'Tera. We are going to visit Mehmet Bay.

The pair rushed out of the museum still holding hands as they reached Kaya's car.

'Oh, yes, how was your meeting with Catling?

Before Andrea had time to open her mouth, they were both in the car.

'You can tell me on the way,' said Kaya.

FIVE

Harvesting the carob trees was one job that Mehmet Bay relished. He used a long thick stick to shake the branches and the carob pods would fall to the ground. Half the pods would then be roasted before being pressed and made into a molasses like syrup, pekmez. Mehmet Bay grew a wide variety of crops including olives, almonds, grapes, broad beans, lemons, and oranges. Most of his income came from selling these crops at markets in Lefke or Polis. All the market sellers in Lefke knew Mehmet Bay, his nickname was Gangaro, derived from the fact that he was tall and strong. Ali once told Kaya the story of when Mehmet Bay first visited the market in Lefke, carrying his crops on a horse drawn cart. The traders had to queue and would be allocated a site to pitch by the market inspector, the issue was the inspector was Greek Cypriot and he would allocate the best sites to Greeks and never to the Turkish Cypriot sellers, even if the Turks had been first in the queue. Many of the Turkish sellers from Tera moaned and complained on a regular basis but this fell on deaf ears and this form of racial discrimination continued until the day Mehmet Bay turned up.

Mehmet Bay and two other villagers from Tera, Enver and Halil were the first traders to arrive at the market square. Mehmet Bay pointed to the site pitches at the entrance of the market.

'We will take those pitches,' said Mehmet Bay pulling his horse and cart to the place he wanted.

'Mehmet Bay, you have to wait for the market inspector to allocate you a site,' Enver shouted at Mehmet Bay.

'I understand Enver, we were the first traders here so he will give us first few pitches,' he shouted back.

Other traders started to turn up and were surprised to see the three men from Tera already setting up their stalls. A hullabaloo began to build up as the numbers increased, traders muttering amongst themselves while staring at the men from Tera. Finally, the market inspector turned up and the Greek traders all rushed him pointing furiously at the Turks. The Inspector marched over and was met by Mehmet Bay who stood in front of him.

'You have to move from here,' the Inspector blurted out.

Mehmet Bay, who towered over him, smirked.

'Why do I have to move? My friends and I were the first traders on site therefore we should have choice of where to set up our stalls,' Mehmet Bay calmy said.

'No, I allocate the pitches,' replied the now irritated Inspector.

'Based on what?' questioned Mehmet Bay.

'As the Inspector I have final decision on where each trader can set up their pitch.'

Mehmet Bay took some coins out from his trouser pocket, opened the palm of his hand to show the coins to the Inspector before putting them in the inspector's jacket outside pocket.

'My understanding and the understanding of my friends is that this market has always operated on a first come first serve basis, therefore we were here first so we have first choice. I have just paid you the pitch fees for me and my two friends. Buyers are beginning to turn up so you should help the other traders,' Mehmet Bay informed the Inspector pointing towards the entrance of the market and to the large queue of people that was building up.

With a huff and a puff the Inspector marched off to speak to the other traders. By the time the Inspector had a chance to walk over to the other traders the public had entered the market square and naturally the first stall they came to was Mehmet Bay's. Olive oil proved to be the most popular selling item, all six jars sold within half an hour, not surprising considering his price for the oil was considerably cheaper than the olive oil sold at the local shops in Lefke. Enver and Halil resembled Cheshire cats that had just licked an overflowing plate of cream after making more money in one day than ever before. Carob and broad beans were the other most popular crops with buyers so Mehmet Bay sold out on these items.

'We have to come again on Friday, normally much busier than today,' Enver spoke out loud.

'I may have to bring two carts,' said Mehmet Bay breaking out in rare smile.

As the men from Tera were packing away a group of five Greek traders walked up to them.

'Well done, you all had a good day. We have no problem today, but if you ever come back to this market again you will have a lot of trouble,' said one of the traders.

Mehmet Bay walked up to trader who had given them the warning.

'Is that a threat?'

The trader stepped back, not just in fright but also from the pungent smell of Mehmet Bay's breath, a consequence of eating two raw cloves of garlic every morning. Mehmet Bay turned round to Enver and Halil.

'Let's go Home.'

Friday morning came and Mehmet Bay, Enver and Halil were again the first traders to turn up at the market and again they set up at the entrance of the market. Anticipating that this would happen the Greek traders had hired someone, a type of enforcer, to warn off the men from Tera. The enforcer, a stocky man with a noticeable limp, walked over to the men.

'You are not welcome here, I want you to leave the market,' ordered the enforcer.

Mehmet Bay nonchalantly put the jars of olive oil on the ground, today he had ten jars to sell.

'Who are you ordering us what to do?' bellowed out Mehmet Bay.

'The traders have hired me to get you out.'

Mehmet Bay laughed out loud.

'Let me understand this. They have paid you money to stop us selling our crops at the market,' Mehmet Bay yelled.

The enforcer grabbed Mehmet Bay's arm.

Mehmet Bay in turn pushed the enforcer's hand away, grabbed the top of his shirt, violently twisted him like a ragdoll and pinned him against the side of his cart. A knife fell from the enforcer's pocket.

'I think you should be the one who leaves the market,' Mehmet Bay told him in no uncertain terms.

He then threw the enforcer to the ground, picked up the knife and put it into his own pocket. The enforcer sluggishly got to his feet, looking more embarrassed than anything else he walked towards a group of the traders.

'Why didn't any of you come and help me,' he shouted at the traders.

'That's why we paid you,' came the response from one of the traders.

'If I were you, I would ask for my money back,' Mehmet Bay shouted at the traders.

After that day many more villagers from Tera would travel to the market in Lefke to sell their goods and Mehmet Bay became known as Gangaro. No one asked him the leave the market ever again, indeed anyone from Tera were always given the best pitches.

Kaya and Andrea were driving to Tera.

'I heard about the shooting in the village,' Andrea said as she linked her arm to his.

'Very fortunate that no one got killed. My father was at the café at the time so he could have been shot. They were after Sergeant Yilmaz. That is way I am really worried how the troubles are escalating. EOKA are now targeting Turkish Cypriots and the Turks are beginning to arm themselves. Do you have any ideas why EOKA are targeting Turks?

'Their struggle is with the British so I do not know why they seem to be attacking Turks. Maybe, they see that the police force is totally Turkish Cypriot and that the Turks are collaborating with the British,' Andrea made the point.

'Maybe, but all it is resulting in is pushing the two communities apart. Animosity is growing day by day.'

'We have had this conversation before, the best solution is for the British to withdraw and for the Island to be Independent and declared a Republic,' Andrea said forthrightly.

'I know, but some factions within EOKA, and even Archbishop Makarios, want enosis with Greece, but that is not acceptable for the Turkish people on the Island. After independence who guarantees the safety of the Turkish Cypriots?'

'Why would Turkish Cypriots want safety? In a Republic Greeks and Turks would live and work in harmony ensuring the future prosperity of the Island,' said Andrea.

'But would they?' questioned Kaya.

'Would they what?'

'Live side by side in harmony. My uncle was murdered by EOKA gunman, and my father could also have been killed the other night. When these people come into power do you just forgive and forgot?

'I am sorry about your uncle but things will be different once the British leave. Maybe that is their goal to drive a wedge between our two communities?'

Kaya turned to her and nodded.

'I am beginning to believe that you are correct. Dividing the communities only benefits the British, planting several seeds that would eventually lead to conflict. Once they eventually depart would they care what happens to the Island?' he asked directly looking at Andrea.

Andrea's stern face kept staring forwards.

'What is Christo's view?'

'Why do you want to know?' she said with a puzzled expression.

'Come on you must have discussed this, I am sure boyfriend and girlfriend talk about these types of things it's not just about the sex,' remarked Kaya taking her by surprise.

'We are not boyfriend and girlfriend,' she snapped back.

'Have you told him that we are in a relationship?' he asked.

'You do understand that a Greek woman having a relationship with a Turkish man is taboo. No, I have not told anybody about us,' she confirmed.

'I understand and know it is taboo, but have we not just

spoken about our two communities living in harmony? My parents would never accept me marrying a Greek girl. But for cultures to exist together is that what would need to occur? Do mixing different cultures and ethnic groups infer more understanding, more harmony? I do not know the answer.'

Kaya and Andrea arrived at Mehmet Bay's house. The front door was closed so they walked around the side to the back of the house, to find Mehmet Bay sat on a chair with his feet up on a stool. Audible snoring proving that he was fast asleep. A nap during the day was essential for someone who woke at five o'clock every morning.

'What should we do?' asked Andrea.

'He is bound to wake up soon. We'll just wait here,' said Kaya as he quietly walked over to a chair and sat down opposite Mehmet Bay. He beckoned over Andrea pointing to a chair next to him. She walked over but stumbled on the uneven ground and fell forwards, Kaya reacted standing up and catching her.

'What's going on?' shouted Mehmet Bay waking up to the commotion.

'Hello Mehmet Bay, sorry to disturb you but we have some questions we would like to ask you,' Kaya said with trepidation, unsure what his reaction would be.

Mehmet Bay was disorientated for a moment or two before realising who the two people in front of him were. A man in his fifties his craggily face made him look ten years older, but physically he was fitter and stronger than most men half his age.

'Sit down. What do you want to ask me?

'How long have oranges been grown on your land?' asked Kaya.

'My grandfather, Haji Hodja, planted the first orange trees. He had first seen oranges on a farm while traveling to Polis and he stopped and picked a couple and ate them. Amazed by the taste he asked the farmer where he had acquired the trees from and was told a man in Polis was selling young orange trees. At the time most farmers including Haji Hodja grew olives, but a disease had swept through this part of the Island wiping out a huge number of olive trees. Haji Hodja cut them all down and burnt them, bought several orange trees and planted them either side of the stream. The trees flourished, mainly due to the soil and watering them constantly, especially in the summer,' explained Mehmet Bay.

'Did your grandfather start planting the orange trees before the fountain in the Village?' Andrea asked.

Mehmet Bay scrunched up his face as he thought about it for a moment.

'I believe it was around the same time.'

Kaya and Andrea glanced at each other.

'Could Haji Hodja read and write Arabic? Kaya asked.

'Why are you asking me these questions?'

Kaya hesitated for a moment.

'We found an inscription on one of the stones of the fountain written in Arabic and was wondering if Haji Hodja could have written it?' asked Andrea jumping in ahead of Kaya.

'My grandfather was a Hodja, a teacher and practicing Muslim, the Imam of the village, so he could read and write in Arabic. Did I ever tell you when he went on the Haj pilgrimage to Mecca. He sailed to the Levant before making his way to Damascus before joining the pilgrimage route to Mecca. In those days pilgrims traveled with a camel caravan for weeks upon weeks in the hot searing desert before reaching Mecca. It took him three months to go to Mecca and return. I am not a practicing Muslim, but I respect what my grandfather did. He paid for the building of the fountain in 1904 and this benefited the whole village. Even today people still use the fountain.'

Kaya and Andrea looked duly impressed.

'In answer to you question I do not know if he wrote the inscription. I have never noticed it. What does it say?' asked Mehmet Bay.

'A tribute is dedicated to Tera and the future prosperity of the village lies under the orange trees,' Kaya told him.

'What is a tribute?'

'Usually, an amount of money or anything else of value given on the behalf of someone.'

Mehmet Bay stared into the sky, pondering Kaya's explanation.

'Is it something to do the with the Roman coin? We spoke about this before. I have only ever found one coin but are you saying there is more?' said Mehmet Bay.

'Possibly. You have dug there, and we have dug there without finding any more. My only conclusion is maybe someone found them before and maybe buried them elsewhere,' said Kaya.

'Under the orange trees,' Mehmet Bay said before repeating it a few times.

He shook his head as he got up.

'No, I do not know,' he said as Kaya and Andrea also got up.

'Anyway, thank you for your time,' Kaya said as he went to leave.

'Thank you, Mehmet Bay,' said Andrea.

'Wait! My grandfather did build a water well in the middle

of the orange trees, but it has long been dry.'

Kaya and Andrea suddenly turned around when they heard that.

'If you want, I can take you there?' Offered Mehmet Bay.

'Yes, if you do not mind? Said Kaya.

Mehmet Bay set a relentless pace, Kaya and Andrea struggled to keep up with him. Through the carob trees and round the almonds and straight past the broad beans before they reached the orange groves. Mehmet Bay suddenly stopped.

'This is the well,' he said pointing towards the ground to a large wooden board that covered a square in between two trees.

Kaya and Andrea stood around it.

'When was the last time it was used?' asked Andrea.

'I remember opening it up over ten years ago to check if there was any water, but it was dry. I never understood why my grandfather built it as he received ample water from the stream.'

'How deep is it?'

'Let's find out,' Mehmet Bay said as he lifted two large stones that held the board in place. Kaya helped him lift the heavy board. Mehmet Bay found a small stone and dropped it down the well and all that was heard was a thud as it landed on solid earth.

'Kaya, if you want to bring your equipment, I will help you dig the bottom of the well. You probably will not find anything but at least you have investigated it,' said Mehmet Bay.

Kaya was taken by surprised by the offer.

'Thank you, Mehmet Bay,' he said looking at his watch.

'Go and get your equipment.'

'If you do not mind Mehmet Bay.'

'No, I'll wait for you.'

In a flash Kaya and Andrea headed for the land rover. They rushed back with rope, a shovel, a battery-operated lantern, and a trowel.

'Give me the rope,' said Mehmet Bay grabbing one end of the rope and tying it around the trunk of an orange tree.

Kaya tied the other end round his waist, placed the shovel between the rope and his waist and carried the lantern.

'I will hold the rope and lower you down,' instructed Mehmet Bay.

'Are you going to be alright?' Andrea whispered to Kaya.

'Yes, I'll be fine.

'Whenever you are ready Mehmet Bay.'

Mehmet Bay nodded his head and held the rope firmly. Kaya stepped to the edge of the well and Mehmet Bay gradually loosened the rope allowing Kaya to lower himself into the well. It was approximately twenty feet down and he switched on the lantern before reaching the bottom of the well.

'I am at the bottom,' he shouted.

Kaya untied himself.

'I will start digging.'

He began to start digging the ground at the bottom of the well. The ground was rock hard but once Kaya had dug the top layer the soil became softer and, in some places, moist. Andrea and Mehmet Bay observed Kaya from above, both on their knees perched on the edge of the well. Then a sudden thud echoed from the bottom of the well.

'What is it?' shouted Mehmet Bay.

Kaya had hit a metal object with the shovel. He frantically carried on digging wiping the soil off the metal surface with his hands. He stood up and lifted the lantern up.

'It is a metal box.'

'How big is it?' shouted down Andera.

'I would estimate its two foot by one foot and about one foot deep. It is too heavy for me to lift,' replied Kaya.

'Let me get another rope,' said Mehmet Bay before setting off to the van.

'Can you open it?' Andrea shouted down to Kaya.

'It has two handles at either end and a kind of latch on top. We need to lift it before we can try and open it,' said Kaya.

Mehmet Bay came back with another rope and threw one end of it down to Kaya.

'Tie both ropes around the box. You can then climb up and we will both pull it up,' said Mehmet Bay as he tied the end of the second rope around the trunk of an orange tree.

Kaya found it too difficult to tie the ropes underneath the box, so he tied the end of the ropes to the metal handles on the box.

'I am going to climb up,' shouted out Kaya.

Mehmet Bay pulled both ropes to make them taut using the metal box in the well as a base. Kaya held the ropes and tentatively climbed up the side of the well and out.

'The box is very heavy,' said Kaya.

'We'll manage,' added Mehmet Bay with reassurance.

Andrea gave both the men a pair of gloves each. Mehmet Bay held one rope and Kaya and Andrea held the other.

'Are you ready?' asked Mehmet Bay.

'We'll start pulling on your command,' answered Kaya.

'Pull!'

All three of them started to pull and Mehmet Bay dug his boots in the ground to give him extra support. The box appeared and got stuck at the top edge of the well. Mehmet rushed forward and pulled it out. Kaya used a brush to remove and soil and Andrea poured water on it from her canister and used a cloth to wipe the top. Mehmet Bay examined the latches, and both had rusted.

'Can you get me a hammer and a chisel?'

Andrea nodded and went to the van to get a bag of tools.

'If we can undo the latches the top panel of the box slides open,' explained Mehmet Bay.

Andrea handed a hammer and chisel to Mehmet Bay who wasted no time in trying to prize open the latches. Gradually they loosened and he was able to slide open the top panel of the box to reveal another wooden panel underneath. Mehmet Bay use the chisel to lift the panel from the side. All three took a step back and froze, awestruck by the contents of the box. Dozens, indeed, hundreds of gold coins. Kaya stepped forward and picked up one of the coins and rubbed it and the coin glistened, as quite clearly visible was the head of Hadrian on the coin.

'This is it,' proclaimed Kaya.

Andrea picked up a coin and so did Mehmet Bay. For a moment or two there was sheer silence as all three of them examined and admired the gold coins.

'How many do you think there is?' asked Andrea.

Mehmet Bay put his hand all the way into the box.

'I would say a few hundred, but we need to count them,' Mehmet Bay recommended.

'Yes, but we need take the box somewhere before we count them,' responded Kaya.

'My house is the nearest we can take the box there,' Mehmet Bay insisted.

'It is too heavy to carry,' Kaya said.

'I will bring Lokum, he will help us carry it.'

'Lokum?' said Andrea with a quizzical look.

'He is my donkey. I also have a small cart we could put

the box on. It is small enough to fit through the trees.'

Mehmet Bay flicked the gold coin he was holding back into the box and marched off. Kaya turned to Andrea and held her hand.

'We found it. I cannot believe it. This must rank as one of the most important archaeological finds in Cyprus,' Kaya said to her.

'In terms of value I think it is the biggest find ever,' confirmed Andrea.

'We must phone the museum immediately and inform Mr Catling and Mr Megaw or we take the coins back to museum,' pondered Kaya.

'It is too late to drive there today. We will take the coins to Mehmet Bay's house, count them and leave them there for the night and take them first thing in the morning,' suggested Andrea.

'Most sensible,' Kaya said agreeing with her suggestion.

They both sat by the metal box shifting through the coins.

'You do know what this mean?' said Andrea.

'No.'

'Fame. Every paper in Cyprus and even from around the World will want to interview you. The man who found Hadrian's gold. A hair cut would be a good idea before the reporters and photographers start arriving,' suggested Andrea.

'What's wrong with my hair?' Kaya said as he ran his hand through his long uncombed hair.

'Nothing,' she said as she leant over and kissed him.

'If you're not going back tonight you can spend the night at my house,' he proposed.

'I am not going to get a better offer than that,' Andrea said as they continued kissing.

A clatter of hooves drew closer and closer. Andrea

stood up tucking her shirt into her trousers. Kaya rubbed the dust off his trousers. Mehmet Bay appeared from the trees pulling along Lokum the donkey and a small cart. Kaya slid the metal panel to close the box, while Andrea started patting Lokum.

'Andrea, we are going to also need your help to lift the box onto the cart,' Mehmet Bay called out to her.

All three stood around the box.

'Lifting it off the ground is easy but lifting it onto the cart is the problem,' said Mehmet Bay.

Kaya and Mehmet Bay lifted the box from each end and Andrea held the bottom of the box from the middle.

'One last effort,' urged Mehmet Bay.

They lifted the box onto the edge of the cart and all three of them pushed it onto the cart.

'Come on lokum, let's go home,' Mehmet Bay said as he slapped the donkey's backside.

The slap had an opposite effect and made Lokum go slowly rather than quicker.

Finally, they reached the house and Mehmet Bay opened the barn door and led Lokum into it. He untied Lokum from the cart and led him outside. Kaya and Andrea lifted a table and put it next to the cart. A short while later Mehmet Bay brought with him three chairs.

'We better start counting the coins. The best way is to put them in stacks of ten coins,' suggested Kaya.

Mehmet Bay grabbed two handfuls of coins and placed them on the table in front of him and started counting. Andrea followed suit. Kaya took out a notebook, pen and ruler and put them down on the table. He picked up just one coin and started to measure its diameter.

'I hope you are not going to measure each coin?' Mehmet Bay remarked.

Kaya looked at Mehmet Bay and smiled and wrote down the measurement of the coin in his notebook. He also wrote down the inscription of the gold aureus. On one side of the coin the inscription read: IMP CAESAR TRAIAN HADRIANVS AVG with a laureate, draped and cuirassed bust of Hadrian looking right. On the reverse the inscription read P M TR P COS III, with the figure of Jupiter seated left on a backless throne, holding thunderbolt upward and vertical scepter.

'How much would one of these coins be worth?' asked a curious Mehmet Bay.

'When I was in England, a coin very similar to this sold in auction for nearly five hundred British pounds,' Kaya confirmed.

Kaya's comment made Mehmet Bay sit upright.

Stack after stack built up until all the coins had disappeared from the metal box. Kaya tried to lift the metal box but it was still heavy.

'I think it was the actual box that was heavy and not the coins inside,' said Kaya.

Andrea started to count the stacks.

'One hundred, two hundred, three hundred, four hundred. The final amount is 487 coins.' Andrea reported.

'That is a fortune,' uttered Kaya.

'What are your plans?' Mehmet Bay enquired.

'Mehmet Bay, if you do not mind can we leave the coins here overnight and tomorrow we will take them to the Museum,' said Kaya.

'I have a lock for the barn and I will put the key under my pillow tonight,' he told Kaya.

They put all the coins back into the box and left the barn. Mehmet Bay locked the door with a padlock and held the key up before putting it in his trouser pocket.

'Andrea and I are going to drive to Kritou and phone the museum,' Kaya informed Mehmet Bay.

The journey to Kritou was short and the streets were empty as Kaya drove to the café located in the center of the village. All eyes diverted to Andrea as the pair walked into the café. Andrea sat down at a table as Kaya went into the back room to make the phone call to the Museum. The café owner brought over a cup of Turkish coffee, a glass of water and a piece of Turkish Delight. Andrea felt uncomfortable as all eyes were still fixated with her.

'What are you all looking at?' the café owner said in a raised voice. All the men looked away, some playing backgammon whilst others chatted amongst themselves.

Kaya returned and sat down next to Andrea.

'I spoke to Mr Catling and told him of our discovery, and he thought I was making a joke, but once I convinced him he ran to Mr Megaw's office and they are both coming to Tera first thing tomorrow morning.'

'I did not expect anything from them. Any major discovery and they both turn up the next day,' Andrea explained.

'They want to see the place the coins were discovered and then they will take the coins back to the museum,' said Kaya.

'I need to phone my parents and tell them I am staying in Tera tonight.'

She stroked Kaya's arm as she got up and walked to the back room.

'Get up, it is six o'clock,' shouted Ali as he banged on Kaya's bedroom door.

Andrea poked Kaya in the side.

'Your dad is outside,' she whispered.

'Oh,' was his only comment.

Both had bleary eyes an indication of very little sleep during the night.

Nalan was preparing breakfast, fresh eggs collected from the hen coop. Ali walked in triumphantly.

'A big day for the village today and an even bigger day for our son. It is not every day that the village you live in is the site of one of the biggest discoveries of treasure on the Island,' he boasted.

Kaya walked into the kitchen closely followed by Andrea.

'Andrea, I didn't know you were spending the night,' Nalan said whilst staring intently at Kaya.

'There was no point in her going home and coming back this morning. Mr Catling and Mr Megaw are arriving this morning,' explained Kaya.

'Where did you sleep? You weren't in the spare room,' asked a suspicious Nalan.

'I did not want to be a burden to you again. I know you were kind enough to give me somewhere to sleep during the excavation, but this was an unannounced stay, so I slept in Kaya's bed, and he slept on the floor,' said Andrea.

Nalan looked at Ali who shrugged his shoulders.

Mehmet Bay had set the table outside awaiting the arrival of his guests. His wife had baked fresh pancakes and jars of homemade pekmez. Honey and marmalade adorned the table with pots of tea.

'It seems I have arrived just in time.'

Mehmet Bay turned around to see his son, Sergeant Yilmaz, standing by the table dipping a pancake into a jar of pekmez.

'Those are for our guests.'

'What guests dad?

'People from the museum are coming.'

'Is this for the Roman Treasure?'

'How do you know about it?' asked Mehmet Bay.

'We received a call from the museum saying that gold Roman coins were discovered in Tera. We need to log it down and confirm the nature of the treasure.' Yilmaz explained.

Mehmet Bay unlocked the barn door and walked over to the metal box that was on the cart and slid the top panel open. Yilmaz was taken aback and picked up one of the coins.

'Amazing,'

Kaya and Andrea arrived.

'Phew,' exclaimed Andrea.

Kaya gave a puzzled glance.

'I am relived, the coins are still here,' she said.

Soon after Catling and Megaw arrived accompanied by a reporter and photographer from the Cyprus Mail. Even though it was warm day Megaw wore a three-piece stripey suit with a flowery tie.

'How many coins are there?' he asked.

As Kaya was just about to open his mouth.

'Four hundred, sir,' interrupted Mehmet Bay.

Kaya and Andrea looked at each other in amazement.

'I thought there was well over four hundred,' Magaw turned to Catling who in turn looked at Kaya.

'I think we should count them again,' said Kaya.

'Great idea,' said the reporter.

'We can take some photographs during the count,' said the photographer.

Kaya and Andrea started counting the coins again under the watchful eyes of Megaw and Catling.

The photographer taking photos of each of them.

'Four hundred,' stated Kaya.

Catling counted the stacks of ten coins.

'Yes, I can confirm there is exactly four hundred coins,' said Catling.

'I would like to go and see the location of the find,' requested Megaw.

Kaya stood up and led the way grabbing Mehmet Bay's arm on the way.

'Where is the rest of the coins? There was four hundred and eighty seven and now there is only four hundred,' Kaya angrily asked.

'Have you forgotten what the inscription on the fountain said? It is now for the future prosperity of the village. I have taken it for the village and not for my personnel gain. I will record everything that I spend and give you a regular update,' Mehmet Bay said quietly so no one else heard.

The entourage arrived at the well and the photography started taking photographs of everyone.

Andrea approached Kaya.

'What are we going to do about Mehmet Bay? We cannot just let him take the coins.'

'I will deal with the situation,' said Kaya trying to re-assure her.

'I have seen some amazing artifacts discovered on this Island, but this must be the greatest,' Megaw told the reporter.

After yet more photographs everyone walked back to Mehmet Bay's house. The metal box of coins was lifted into Kaya's van. Megaw and Catling bid farewell to Mehmet Bay and his family.

'I can escort you to Polis and then I will have to leave you. From there drive to Morphou and then onto Lefkosa,' Yilmaz said to Kaya.

As Yilmaz walked to his motorcycle, Andrea nudged Kaya in the side.

'Should we not tell Sergeant Yilmaz about the coins?'

'Tell him that his father stole some of coins!' said Kaya sarcastically.

Yilmaz on his motorcycle led the way followed by Kaya and Andrea in the van carrying the box of coins and Megaw and Catling following behind in Catling's car. The reporter continued interviewing Mehmet Bay.

Tera to Polis was a relatively short journey by car and as Yilmaz came up to the junction, he stopped allowing Kaya to drive next to him.

'I will have to leave you here,' said Yilmaz.

'Thank you, Sergeant Yilmaz. I will see you soon.'

The van turned right, and Yilmaz raised his hand to Catling and Megaw as they followed the van. The road ahead was clear until they came to an army checkpoint. A soldier gesticulated to Kaya to stop and he duly complied.

'Where are you traveling to?' asked the solider in a broad Irish accent.

'We are going to Nicosia and so is the car behind us. We all work at the Archaeological Museum.'

The soldier walked to Catling's car.

'Are you with the van front?'

'Yes,' responded Catling.

Megaw took out a piece of paper and handed it to the soldier, who read it and gave a salute.

'Open the barrier, they can go through,' the soldier shouted to the two other soldiers by the barrier who opened the barrier for the van and car to continue their journey.

A few miles further on and Kaya could see a truck in the road ahead and as he got closer the truck was stationary. Kaya slowed down and was preparing to overtake when a car came from the opposite direction and suddenly stopped next to the truck forcing Kaya to stop the van Catling stopped behind the van.

'What is going on?' said Kaya.

Suddenly four armed men all dressed in black ran towards the car and van.

'Get Out! Get Out!' shouted one of the gunmen.

One of the others opened the driver's door and pulled Kaya out the van.

'On the ground, lay flat on the ground.'

The gunman then tied Kaya's hand behind his back and put a blindfold on him.

'Get up.'

The gunman pulled up Kaya and led him to the back of the truck before he was put into the truck and forced to sit on a bench.

'Who are you?' shouted Kaya.

'EOKA!' came the response.

SIX

Soldiers from the Royal Ulster Rifles swarmed all over the abandoned van and car. The doors of the van Kaya was driving were open as was the drivers' and the passenger doors of Catling's car. Sergeant Yilmaz paced up and down between the van and car. The doors at the back of the van were also open and Yilmaz looked in to confirm the inevitable, the disappearance of the Roman gold coins, noting it down in his well-used notebook. A police land rover arrived, and Inspector Tapping stepped out of the passenger side. Autumn winds had calmed the temperature, but it was still far too hot for Tapping who removed his peaked cap to wipe away the sweat from his forehead before wearing it again. Tapping was the commending officer of the Mobile Reserve Police unit based at the Limni camp, near Polis.

'Sergeant, I cannot stay too long, news of the abductions has broken and Major Scott has informed me that the Governor is on his way to the camp. In fact, I want you to come with me as I am making you the lead officer on this,' Tapping informed Yilmaz.

'Yes Sir, thank you sir,' Yilmaz replied apprehensively.

'Who was in the Van?' asked Tapping.

'Kaya Mustafa was driving the van and Andrea Polyanidis was in the passenger seat and the metal box of Roman gold coins was in the back.'

'Now, these Roman coins, how many are we talking about?'

'Sir, we are talking a fortune,' Yilmaz told him.

'Do you think then they were after the coins?'

'Without a doubt Sir, but how would they have known the time and the route?' Yilmaz posed to Tapping.

'We may know the answer to that, Sergeant. We have an Intelligence Officer at the Museum in Nicosia, and he has provided some important information.'

'Mr Megaw and Mr Catling were following in the car behind. There is no sign of any blood or shots being fired so we must assume they are being held captive somewhere,' said Yilmaz.

'Come on we must head back to the camp before the Governor arrives,' Tapping ordered.

'Sorry Sir, but I wanted to go to Tera and inform Kaya's family what has happened. He is the nephew of the late Sergeant Hasan Mustafa,' explained Yilmaz.

'Oh, you can go but I want you back at the camp as soon as possible thereafter.'

'Yes, Sir.'

Ali was loading his cart with crates of potatoes that he had dug up that morning in preparation for his journey to Lefke the next morning to sell them at the market. The sound of the motorcycle alerted him of Yilmaz's pending arrival. He grabbed a handful of potatoes and placed them in a basket situated on the outside table. Yilmaz pulled in and stopped by the cart.

'Just in time,' Ali said lifting the basket of potatoes, preparing to hand it to Yilmaz.

Yilmaz walked up to him. Ali put down the basket sensing something was wrong.

'Ali Bay, I must tell you that we found the van Kaya was driving abandoned on the road just outside Polis. Kaya, Andrea, Mr Megaw and Mr Catling are all missing, as is the Roman coins.'

'Was it EOKA?'

'We believe so,' Yilmaz confirmed.

'You should be out there looking for him,' Ali told him.

'British soldiers are searching the near vicinity. We will find him.'

'First my brother, now my son. Is this family cursed?' Ali said slumping to the ground uncontrollably.

Yilmaz helped him to his feet.

'Ali Bay, I will find him and bring him back home.'

Ali nodded, tears streaming down his face.

'I pray to Allah that you do,' Ali said grasping Yilmaz's hand.

'We must and we will act now,' Ali said wiping away his tears with a handkerchief.

'No,' Yilmaz vehemently said shaking his head.

'Yilmaz, you know the only way to protect ourselves is to stand and fight.'

'Fight who?' questioned Yilmaz.

'Fight for our right of self-determination, when the British finally leave we cannot let the Greeks rule us. They already think they are superior to us, but they will get a rude awakening one day. Denktaş and Vuruşkan are right we must arm ourselves and be prepared to protect our homes and villages. If EOKA started to kill members of your family would you not fight back?' asked Ali.

'I would find them and make sure they stand trial,' replied Yilmaz.

'You must be a better man than me,' Ali told him.

'I am no better than anyone else Ali Bay. I am just trying to do my job and keep my family safe. I have to accept that my life is at risk every time I walk outside the camp but I made that choice and have to live with it. Cyprus is in an absolute mess. Would it be any better if the British leave and the Island gains independence? I wish I could look into the future and know what would happen that would dictate how I live my life now.'

Ali continued grasping Yilmaz's hand.

'You are a good and wise man, but I beg you please find my son please,' he pleaded.

Yilmaz nodded and let go of his hand.

'I must go Ali Bay.'

'May Allah grant you speed,' said Ali as Yilmaz mounted his motorcycle.

Soldiers at the camp located at Limni, on the outskirts of Polis, were preparing for the imminent visit of the Governor of Cyprus. One of the Sergeant Majors was yelling out orders to anyone in earshot. To Sergeant Major O'Connell of the Royal Ulster Rifles, the visit from the Governor was an inconvenience. The regiment was in the process of relocating their camp from Limni to Kykko and the logistics of moving a whole battalion was giving the Sergeant Major many sleepless nights. Limni was also the temporary home of the Mobile Reserve Unit, the two armed soldiers on sentry opened the barrier and waived through Yilmaz who had arrived on his motorcycle. After dismounting he headed straight to Inspector Tapping's office. Tapping was in mid conversation with Sergeant Ferdi when Yilmaz knocked and came in.

'Yilmaz, good timing, we have just been informed that the truck seen near the scene of the abductions was sighted heading towards the village of Tala near Paphos,' Tapping pronounced in an excitable voice.

'I know the village Sir,' replied Yilmaz.

'Any idea why they would take the captives there?' asked Tapping.

'Yes, St. Neophytos monastery is about a mile north of Tala. The monastery is built into a natural cave, therefore it is very difficult to approach without being seen. The best element of surprise would be to ascend from the top of the caves,' recommended Yilmaz.

'Good, lets get some plain clothes officers there immediately. Ferdi, get seven or eight men to stake it out. We need to be certain they are being held there,' ordered Tapping.

'I will go right away, sir' Ferdi said on his way out of the room.

'Stay in contact.' Tapping shouted as Ferdi closed the door behind him.

Tapping then produced a large brown envelope from his desk drawer opened it taking out several photographs.

'As I mentioned, we have an intelligence officer at the Museum in Nicosia and these are photographs of suspected EOKA members he has taken.'

Tapping placed the photographs in front of Yilmaz, but at that precise moment there was a knock on the door and a soldier stepped in.

'Sir, Field Marshall Harding and Major Scott,' bellowed out the soldier as he gave salute.

Harding and Scott walked in. Tapping and Yilmaz stood and gave salute. Yilmaz swiftly moved the two chairs so there was ample room for the men to sit down. The soldier closed the door and stood in front of it.

'Field Marshall, this is Inspector Tapping who commands the Mobile Reserve at Limni and this is Sergeant Yilmaz. Sergeant Yilmaz captured the EOKA gunmen who were responsible for the murder of the Policeman in Tera,' introduced Major Scott.

Scott was the Commanding Officer of the Mobile Reserve

Corps in Cyprus, another World War II veteran like Harding.

'Excellent effort Sergeant,' said Harding.

'Thank you, Sir,' said Yilmaz giving a salute.

'Now, what is the latest on the kidnappings?' Harding said coughing.

Yilmaz noticed that Harding only had two fingers on his left hand.

'The vehicle involved was seen heading to a village called Tala, near Paphos. Sergeant Yilmaz believes they may be hold out in a monastery just north of the village,' Tapping informed them.

'And is Mr Megaw is one of the people abducted?'

'Yes sir, Mr Megaw, his assistant Mr Catling and the two archaeologists who discovered the Roman coins,' said Tapping.

'I know Mr Megaw, he is a good man. How much are these Roman coins worth?' Harding asked.

Tapping looked up to Yilmaz as to prompt him.

'They found four hundred gold coins from the time of the Emperor Hadrian,' said Yilmaz.

Harding started coughing again.

'That's a bloody fortune. If Grivas and his men manage to smuggle the coins out of the Island and sell them on the black market he could fund and arm a whole EOKA battalion. I want every resource we have available in the search for them. They must be found alive, and I also want the EOKA men tried and hanged. I do not know what Grivas is playing at. We negotiate a truce, and he breaks it by killing a Turkish policeman and kidnapping British officials,' said an exasperated Harding.

'We have increased the reward for any information leading to the capture of Grivas to ten thousand British pounds plus passage anywhere in the World,' interjected

Major Scott.

'No one will talk. Why do you think we have hit a brick wall with trying to find him. Anyway, there is something I want to tell you. Not official yet, but I learnt from my time serving in two world wars that you should always tell your men first. I intend to write to the Foreign Office in London to tender my resignation as Governor of Cyprus,' Harding confirmed to the men before more coughing stopped him in mid flow.

Major Scott looked stunned by this piece of news. Yilmaz gave a side glance to Tapping.

'Could I ask why, Sir?' asked Scott.

'I have had this bout of influenza for an eternity, and I cannot seem to be rid of it. My wife has also been ill, so I think the time is right to return to England. I was sent here to quell the Cypriot insurgents and I must admit not everyone agrees with my methods, but the powers that be in London have altered their stance and they want to start negotiating with the Cypriots, and to be frank that is not my cup of tea. No doubt after I leave London will send some Whitehall mandarin to deal with it. The EOKA flame of Enosis will be extinguished, and the dream of union with Greece replaced by independence.'

'Grivas will never accept that,' interrupted Scott.

'No, he will not but our friend the archbishop will. My past interactions with Makarios have shown me that he craves power. Do you honestly believe he would turn down becoming President of a new republic? Moving forward the main problem I see is the deterioration in relations between the Greek and Turkish Cypriots.

Sergeant you are a Turkish Cypriot what do you think?' Harding asked Yilmaz.

'Yes Sir, one of the archaeologists that has been abducted is a Turkish Cypriot from my village. His uncle was the police officer who was killed by EOKA. Many of the Turks in my village want to arm themselves.'

'That is a colossal issue, Sergeant. If Turks and Greeks engage in armed conflict the future of the island is in peril. Off the record I would not blame the Turks if they armed themselves. I served in Gallipoli so I know first hand how tough Turkish armed forces are, I personally would not trust the Greeks,' said Harding.

'Our intelligence has uncovered that certain people known to us are forming some kind of Turkish resistance group that advocate violence against the Greeks,' Scott informed them.

'Unfortunately, I do not know the solution. I will leave it to someone much smarter and with more energy than me to find it. We have digressed let's get back to the job in hand. Inspector, so you think you have discovered where the people from the Museum have been taken?'

'Yes, sir. We also have photographs of suspected EOKA members,' said Tapping as he showed Harding and Scott the five photos on his desk.

Harding glanced through them. One of the photographs caught Yilmaz's eye and he leant over to take a closer look.

'Sir, may I,' Yilmaz asked pointing to the photograph.

'Go ahead,' said Tapping.

Yilmaz picked up the photo and his face froze.

'What is it, Sergeant?' asked Tapping.

'Sir, I know this person,' Yilmaz informed them before pausing.

'Well, who is it?' snapped Tapping.

'It is one of the archaeologists. I know him as Christos. He was part of the excavation team at the Roman site. Kaya and Andrea, two of the people abducted, were also part of the team,' Yilmaz explained.

'Round him up and make him talk,' yelled Harding.

'Yes sir,' Tapping said.

'Major, I want you to command the operation to find everyone who has been abducted and find them alive. I do not care at what expense, ceasefire or not, the ends justify the means. I also want all the people in these photographs rounded up and interned,' Harding instructed.

'Who knows, maybe one of them will lead us to Grivas!' said Tapping.

Harding and Scott glanced at each other.

'We know where Grivas is hiding,' Harding proclaimed.

The comment took Tapping and Yilmaz by surprise.

'If we know where his hideout is why have we not captured him?' asked a confused Tapping,

'It suits us to keep him where he is, intelligence have him under surveillance twenty four hours a day. We monitor who goes in and who comes out of his hideout. Look if we captured him what would we do with him? Execute him? Exile him? Whatever we do with him he would become a martyr in the eyes of the Greeks. If he adheres to the ceasefire he's best placed where he is, if not, we will continue rounding up his minions,' explained Harding.

'But why is there a reward out for his capture of ten thousand pounds?' Tapping asked.

'Oh, that is just a ruse. I would eat my cap if any Greek came forward to inform on him,' said Harding.

There was a knock on the door and a Corporal entered.

'Sorry to disturb you, but I have Major General Kendrew waiting outside,' announced the Corporal.

'Kendrew!' a startled Scott blurted out.

'Yes, I summoned him to join us. Ask him to come in,' said Harding.

Kendrew walked in and Harding, Scott, Tapping and Yilmaz gave salute before Kendrew reciprocated.

Major General Kendrew, a tall, powerfully built man, was the general commanding officer and director of operations in Cyprus. He had been a rugby prop forward and was a member of the 1930 British Lions tour of Australasia.

'Field Marshall, I hear we have located the whereabouts of the four people abducted by EOKA,' said Kendrew.

'Major where is this place again?' asked Harding.

'We believe they may be being held at the St. Neophytos monastery, just north of a village called Tala in Paphos district,' Scott confirmed.

'Do you think they are all alive?' asked Kendrew.

Yes sir. We have sent a reconnaissance unit there and once we have heard from them; we plan to raid the monastery.' Scott informed everyone.

'I would like to join the raid. If that is agreeable with you Field Marshall?' asked Kendrew.

'Actually, I was going to tell the Major that I would like to join the raid on the monastery,' Harding said chuckling to himself.

Harding's chuckling had a domino effect and Kendrew, Scott, followed by Tapping all started laughing. Yilmaz was left perplexed by this demonstration of British humour.

'I suppose the more the merrier,' said Scott.

'Indeed, old boy, indeed,' remarked Kendrew.

The blindfold was untied, and Kaya had to squint to stop the light penetrating his eyes. It took a few seconds for his eyes to become accustomed to the light shining through the high skylight. The walls of the room were covered in Byzantine paintings mainly depicting the Crucifixion of Jesus Christ and other paintings of the

Annunciation, the announcement by the Angel Gabriel to the Virgin Mary that she would conceive a son by the holy spirit, colours still vivid as the day they were painted in the twelfth century. Kaya's hands were tied behind the back of the chair and his ankles were tied behind the chair legs. He turned his head to the side to see Megaw and Catling similarly tied up as a man removed their blindfolds, forcing both men to go through the same issue with their eyes as Kaya endured. The man who removed the blindfolds wore a black shirt and black trousers and then left the room closing the door behind him.

'Where is Andrea?' Kaya asked the others.

'She was put in the back of the truck with us, but I don't know what they have done with her,' Megaw said.

'What are they going to do with us?' asked Catling.

'I have no idea. Hopefully, they just wanted the Roman coins and plan to release us soon,' commented Megaw.

'Where are we?' asked Catling.

'Paintings on the wall suggest a church or monastery. EOKA have used monasteries as hideouts in the past,' Megaw informed them.

'We need to find out what they have done with Andrea,' insisted Kaya.

'I just hope they wanted the Roman coins, and they will release us,' said Catling.

'If only that was the case, but they may have something else planned for us. I just hope I am wrong,' Megaw said as he struggled to undo his tied hands.

The door was unlocked, and three men walked in.

'Who are you?' Megaw asked the men in a raised voice.

'Freedom fighters. Fighting for the freedom of our Island from British imperialism,' said the man in the middle.

'Are you members of EOKA?' asked Megaw.

'Yes,' the man replied.

'What have you done with the girl?' asked Kaya.

'She is safe.'

'Look, I know you are all reasonable men, and I can understand the cause you are fighting for but all three of us are just archaeologists. We are all here to learn about the great history of your people and the history of Cyprus,' Megaw said in very diplomatic fashion.

'No, you are here to steal our history, many artifacts have already been shipped to London. Where were the Roman coins we liberated from you headed for? the EOKA man abruptly said.

'The coins were being transported to the museum in Nicosia, and we wanted to put them on display so that all Cypriots from the Island could come and see them,' explained Megaw.

'What are you going to do with us?' questioned Catling.

'Digenis will let us know,' said the man as they left the room.

'Who is Digenis?' asked Kaya.

'Digenis is the Greek nickname of George Grivas,' Megaw confirmed.

'Do you think Andrea is safe like they say?' asked Kaya.

'I hope so,' replied Megaw.

Staff from the Museum in Nicosia were leaving through the main gate. Christos bid farewell to a couple of colleagues and rushed down the street. As he turned the corner two armed men from the mobile reserve blocked his way and before he had a chance to speak to them, two more men came from behind forcing him against the wall and putting hand cuffs on him. A military van pulled up and he was bundled into the back. Limni Camp was a hive of activity, soldiers from the Royal Ulster Rifles joining the ranks of the mobile reserve. Sergeant Major O'Connell was in his element inspecting the troops. Two vans pulled into the camp and Christos was taken from the back of the second van into the Camp building. He was taken to a small room and strapped to a specially made padded chair by a couple of police officers who turned off the light when they left the room leaving Christos in pitch darkness. Over twenty minutes past before the door opened, Christos looked up, but the door slammed shut   plunging the room into blackness again.

'Where am I? Why have you taken me?' What have I done? Christos emotionally shouted out.

His questions were met with silence.

A bright torch was shone directly in front of his face, almost blinding him, and forcing him to shut his eyes.

'You are a member of EOKA and you are not leaving here until you tell us where your four colleagues have been taken to. Do you know Peter Megaw, Hector Catling, Kaya Mustafa and Andrea Polyandis?' was shouted into the ear of Christos, who was unable to see who was interrogating him.

'I am not a member of EOKA and I work with the people you mentioned,' shouted back Christos.

The torch was switched off and it took Christos a few moments for his eyes to become accustomed to the dark. He could make out two figures moving close to him. The torch was switched on.

'I am not part of EOKA,' insisted Christos.

An object was thrust into his stomach causing him to yell in pain.

'Where are they?'

'Please you have to believe me I have never been a part of

EOKA,' shouted Christos.

The torch was switched off and the men left the room. Christos struggled trying to pull his hands out of the straps on the chair to no avail. The door opened and the room light was switched on. The room became bleary to Christos until he could see a soldier standing in front of him. It was Major Scott.

'Christos, here is the deal. You tell me where your colleagues from the museum are being held and I will open that door and let you walk out of the camp,' Scott said in a very calm fashion.

'I don't know where they are?'

'What is your role within the organization? Asked Scott as he opened the folder he was holding. 'You were at the Roman excavation site near Tera when two British soldiers were killed,' he continued gradually raising his voice.

'I was, that is true, but please believe me I am not part of EOKA. They tried to recruit me, but I refused,' admitted Christos.

'Who tried to recruit you?' Scott asked in an even louder tone.

'A member of EOKA.'

'No good saying to me a member of EOKA. I want a name,' said Scott now shouting.

Christos stayed silent.

'Silence is no good,' said Scott as he opened the door. 'You will have the pleasure of the company of my two officers again,' he said switching off the light on his way out.

The whole interrogation process began again, but this time round the officers used the baton to inflict more damage to

Christos by beating him in the chest and stomach. The officers left the room and Christos shut his eyes in anguish. Scott entered the room soon after.

'Christos, all you need to do to stop this is give me some names, otherwise we will continue all day and all night,' Scott said as he sat in chair opposite Christos.

Scott then got up took the small canister from the side of his belt, opened it, and offered it to Christos.

'Please!' begged Christos, his eyes bloodshot eyes swelling up with tears.

Scott poured water into Christos' mouth.

'I believe you. I don't think you're involved with EOKA, but I want the name of the person who tried to recruit you. No one will ever find out about our conversation.'

Tears began to flow down Christos' cheeks.

'I don't want anyone to hear you say the name. just whisper the name in my ear,' Scott said as he moved his head towards Christos.

Christos whispered in Scott's ear and with that Scott shot up and rushed out of the room.

'What shall we do with him?' one of the officers asked Scott.

'Lock him in a cell for twenty four hours and then let him go,' instructed Scott.

Catling was admiring the paintings on the wall as Megaw maneuvered his chair until he was back-to-back with Kaya's chair until their hands were touching. He then tried to untie Kaya's hands, which proved onerous, but after several minutes he managed to untie Kaya's hands, who untied the rope from his legs, before untying Megaw's hands and legs, who in turn released Catling from his chair. Megaw tried to open the door but to no ones surprise it was locked.

'The Skylight is too high to climb,' Kaya pointed out.

'Our best chance is to pretend we are still tied up, and the next time they come in we overpower them,' Megaw suggested.

'Do you think that is a wise move, since they all seem to be armed,' countered Catling.

'What is your suggestion?' Megaw asked him.

'I said it before maybe they just want the Roman coins.'

'Maybe, but it seems nothing will happen until they hear from Grivas.

'What happens if Grivas says kill them?' Kaya said somberly.

The chirps of crickets greeted the men of the Police mobile reserve as they arrived just outside the St. Neophytos monastery after a seventeen mile journey from Limni. Soldiers from the Royal Ulster Rifles used the cover of darkness to crawl to the edge of the rock face looking down on the monastery buildings. Harding arrived in the unit land rover with Tapping and Yilmaz. Lights illuminated the main church of the monastery known as the Katholikon. Harding gazed at the large Venetian inspired basilica.

'What a splendid building,' said Harding with awestruck admiration.

'Don't worry sir, we will be carful to ensure that there is no damage,' Tapping told the Field Marshall.

Yilmaz was talking on the radio before walking towards Harding and Tapping.

'Sir, Major Scott is on his way, with Major General Kendrew,' Yilmaz informed the men.

'Good, we'll begin the raid once Scott arrives,' said Harding.

The soldiers secured ropes and were preparing to abseil down the rock onto the roof of the monastery. Sergeant Major O'Connell had his men primed and ready. He nudged the soldier lying next to him.

'Lance Corporal, we go when we hear the signal.'

'What's the signal Sir?'

'Lance Corporal, were you at the briefing or were you not?

'I was sir.'

'So, what is the signal?

'A flare?' the Lance Corporal hesitantly said.

'Ten out of ten Lance Corporal,' O'Connell said sarcastically whilst clipping the Corporal's ear.

'Remember Lance Corporal, if one of these EOKA terrorists stand in your way, if in doubt shoot,' O'Connell instructed.

Scott and Kendrew arrived and joined the others.

'Did you bring in Christos?' Harding asked him.

'We did Sir. The bad news is that he is not an EOKA member, but he gave me the name of person who tried to recruit him,' Scott informed everyone.'

'Well,' urged Harding as Yilmaz took a step closer to Scott.

'Andrea.'

Shell shock hit Yilmaz's face.

'That's the girl who was abducted,' Harding said with surprise.

'Tapping is your unit ready?' asked Scott.

'Yes Sir, Sergeant Yilmaz will fire the flare gun to begin the raid,' confirmed Tapping.

'The Ulster Rifles will come from the top. We will make

sure, so no one escapes,' explained Kendrew.

'Well, let's get on with it,' Harding impatiently said.

'Sergeant,' said Tapping looking at Yilmaz.

Yilmaz lifted the flare gun above his head and aimed it in the direction of the monastery and past the rock face and fired it into the air. Four land rovers and a truck sped towards the monastery and stopped in front of the steps on the main entrance. Soldiers cascaded down the rock face onto the roof of the monastery. One of the soldiers pointed to the sky light.

'Down there!' shouted the soldier.

'Look up!' Kaya shouted pointing up to the soldier.

Officers forced open the main door of the monastery. Yilmaz led the charge in and was confronted by a priest dressed in a long black cassock.

'This is the house of god,' the priest said in Greek.

'He's not home tonight,' Yilmaz replied in Greek as he pushed past him.

Tapping and Scott entered the monastery closely followed behind by Harding.

'Don't harm the priests,' Harding shouted from the back.

Soldiers on the roof of the monastery smashed the sky light glass. Shards of glass fell onto Kaya, Megaw and Catling as all three covered their heads with their hands. The Lance Corporal looked down at the men.

'Go on then,' Sergeant Major O'Connell hinted to the Corporal.

With some trepidation the Corporal lowered himself through the sky light and jumped to the floor, falling to his knee.

'Out the way Lance Corporal?' O'Connell yelled.

By the time the Corporal got to his feet, he had to

scrambled to the side to avoid O'Connell jumping on top of him.

As O'Connell landed, his right knee buckled from under him and he fell flat onto the floor. The Corporal rushed to his aid.

'Are you alright Sir?'

O'Connell gingerly got to his feet.

'Yes, a war wound from Korea,' said O'Connell as the Corporal supported him.

'Are you the men they captured?' O'Connell asked.

'Yes,' confirmed Megaw.

They heard the door being unlocked and the Corporal stood in front of the door with rifle pointing forward. Into the room came one of the EOKA men who was startled to see a British solider standing in front of him.

'Take him,' shouted O'Connell to the Corporal.

The Corporal froze. O'Connell rushed past, heavily limping, and hit the EOKA man in the face with the butt of his rifle knocking the man down. Standing in the corridor just outside the room was another EOKA man.

'Do you want some?' shouted O'Connell with such aggression that the man immediately put both hands up.

The police officers rounded up a handful of EOKA men and herded them into the main hall. Harding, Scott, and Kendrew were led to the room that Kaya and the others were being held.

'How are you all? All limbs intact?' Harding said in a frivolous manner.

'Yes, we are all fine,' said Megaw.

'This is one to tell the grandchildren one day,' said Harding.

Tapping and Yilmaz entered the room.

'How did you find us?' asked Catling.

'Someone spotted the truck heading towards the monastery,' said Tapping.

Sergeant Major O'Connell limped back into the room followed by the Lance Corporal and a Private carrying the chest of Roman coins.

'We found it under the alter of the church,' O'Connell informed everyone in the room.

'Under the alter, quite an apt place for it,' said Kendrew.

'Have you found Andrea?' asked an anxious Kaya.

Scott looked at Megaw

'Did you round up Christos?' enquired Megaw.

Tapping and Yilmaz looked at each other with quizzical expressions both thinking how Megaw would know about Christos being a suspected EOKA member. Harding noticed the exchange of looks.

'Let me explain, Mr Megaw is the Director of the Department of Antiquities, he also acts as a Public Information Officer and an Intelligence Officer on behalf the Colonial Government. It was Mr Megaw who provided us with the photographs of the EOKA Suspects,' explained Harding.

'Yes, we brought in Christos and I am adamant that he is not a member or informant for EOKA, but he did tell me the name of the person who tried to recruit him. It was Andrea,' Scott informed everyone.

Kaya was crestfallen.

SEVEN

Strolling through the streets of Limassol on a sunny autumnal day was a pleasant experience. Sounds of the market stall holders selling their wares were reverberating down the main thoroughfare of the city and the smells of the freshly baked breads and the aromas of the olives kept in kegs mixed with garlic and endless baskets filled with fresh fruit and vegetables wafted from the market. Yilmaz and Tapping walked past the central bus station heading towards Kolonakiou Street. They were both dressed in plain clothes.

'Do you have the address?' Tapping asked Yilmaz.

Yilmaz handed Tapping the piece of paper he was holding.

'I think it is the next right,' said Yilmaz.

Tapping looked at the address written down on the piece of paper.

'Yes, this is the street. We want number twenty one,' confirmed Tapping.

Number twenty one was a three story apartment. Tapping knocked three times on the door.

'Who is it?' said someone from inside.

'Tapping and Yilmaz. You are expecting us,' said Tapping.

Yilmaz anxiously looked around to check no one was watching them. The door opened and the pair quickly entered showing their police badges to the officer who opened the door. They walked up three flights to a room on the top floor. Two more police offices greeted them.

'I am Inspector Tapping and this is Sergeant Yilmaz from

the mobile reserve unit based at Limni camp,' Tapping informed the two officers.

'Good to meet you, I am Inspector Harris and this is Sergeant Vural.'

Yilmaz noticed the large pair of binoculars set on a pod close by the window.

'The house in question is the one with the blue door opposite,' said Harris pointing in the direction of the house through the net curtains.

'So, how sure are you that Grivas is hiding there?' Tapping questioned.

'Going by the number of suspected EOKA members going in and out of the house, pretty certain. I have some photographs we have taken over the last few days,' Harris explained as he guided Tapping and Yilmaz to the table in the middle of the room and pointed to the photos laid out on the table.

'Do you recognize any of them?' asked Harris.

Tapping and Yilmaz examined the ten photographs of people entering the house opposite.

Yilmaz pointed at the photograph at the very end and picked it up to show Tapping.

'This is Andrea,' confirmed Yilmaz

'When was this photo taken?' Tapping asked handing the photo to Harris.

Harris looked at Vural.

'Yesterday, we only got the print back this morning,' confirmed Vural.

'When did you see her leave?' Yilmaz asked.

'We work in eight hour shifts so we have the house monitored twenty four hours a day,' explained Harris.

'Let me check the logbook,' said Vural as he opened the book that was kept on a stool by the window. Yilmaz sat on the chair by the window and looked through the binoculars at the house.

'According to the book she has not left.'

'What do you want to do?' Harris asked Tapping.

'Our unit is waiting near the bus station. Once we have her, we are under orders to take her back to Limni. She is implicated in the murder of two British soldiers, the abduction of three archaeologists and the theft of valuable Roman coins, that she unearthed with one of the other archaeologists. We also believe if we had not found the archaeologists EOKA would have executed them,' Tapping informed Harris and Vural.

'Yes, I suppose there is enough there to justify her arrest,' commented Harris.

Tapping and Yilmaz took it in turns with Harris and Vural to watch the house opposite. Tapping took off his light sweater to reveal a revolver strapped to his waist.

'Anyone for tea?' asked Harris.

'I would love a cup,' said Tapping with a smile.

'Not for me,' replied Yilmaz.

Harris was meticulous in preparing a cup of tea from measuring out the right amount of tea leaves to making sure the tea was a certain colour thus equating to its strength.

'Shall I pour?' asked Harris.

'Please do,' said Tapping eagerly awaiting a decent brew.

Yilmaz and Vural looked at each other both grinning at this slice of quintessential Englishness. Harris then fetched a tin of Carnation condensed milk.

'Some people like to put this in their tea,' proclaimed Harris.

'I am not one of those people,' admitted Tapping.

A couple of hours passed until there were some signs of activity.

'Someone is approaching the house,' reported Vural.

The others peaked through the curtains.

'He seems like a delivery driver,' observed Harris.

The door of the house opened, and the delivery man handed over a couple of large boxes, before walking in.

'Do you think that is their weekly grocery shopping?' asked Tapping.

'There!' Vural shouted pointing to the house.

Following the delivery man out of the house was Andrea.

'That's her,' confirmed Yilmaz.

'Let's go!' instructed Tapping grabbing his sweater for the chair and putting it on, Yilmaz was already out the door.

'Thank you for the hospitality. Can you let our unit know,' uttered Tapping as he rushed out trying to keep up with Yilmaz.

Both men left the building and broke out into a jog as they reached the corner of the street.

'Where is she?' called out Tapping.

Both men scanned the street busy with lunchtime crowds.

'Over there!' Yilmaz shouted having spotted Andrea's blue and white scarf she was wearing.

They both began to walk at pace, and it seemed as they were walking against the grain as they zig zagged past people. Yilmaz caught up with her and was following her step by step. Tapping then nudged him.

'Get her,' whispered Tapping.

Yilmaz walked side by side with Andrea and as she turned to him, he grabbed her by the arm.

'Hello Andrea.'

Tapping then grabbed her other arm.

'We need to take you on a little excursion,' Tapping said as they turned right towards the direction of the central bus station.

'Let me go!' she shouted.

'Not possible. We are taking you in for questioning, so you need to come with us,' insisted Tapping.

They soon passed crowds of people waiting for buses.

'Help me! These men are trying to kidnap me!' she screamed in Greek at the top of her voice.

Yilmaz took a firming grip of her arm as all eyes were on the three of them. Andrea then started to struggle forcing Tapping to hold her with both his hands pulling through the crowd.

'Help me! These men are trying to take me,' she continued to shout. Then a man tried to man handle Yilmaz who forcefully pushed him away.

'We are police!' shouted Yilmaz in both English and Greek.

Another group of people blocked their path. Tapping took out his police badge.

'We are police. You need to let us pass,' he shouted brandishing his badge.

Two men appeared from nowhere both holding metal bars.

'Let her go,' ordered one of the men.

A couple of women tried to pull Andrea from the clutches of the men, but Yilmaz pushed them back.

'We are Police offices, do you not understand,' Tapping shouted at the two men holding the metal bars.

'I said let her go,' said one of the men as he moved forward threatening with the metal bar.

'Do not let go of her Sergeant,' Tapping told Yilmaz as he took his revolver out of his holster and fired two shots into the air. This had the desired effect and most of the crowd dispersed apart from the two men with the metal bars who had now been joined by another group of men. At this moment three land rovers drove up and onto the pavement almost knocking over the men with the weapons. Sergeant Ferdi jumped out the first vehicle and fired his sten gun into the ground in front of the group of men. All the men turned and ran.

'Good timing Ferdi,' said Tapping.

They bundled Andrea into one of the land rovers and all three drove off leaving a plume of dust in their wake.

Bleak was the best way to describe the interrogation room at Limni Camp. It contained three substandard chairs and a table that requires a piece of cardboard to be placed under one of the legs to stop it from wobbling. The door was flung open, and two offices brought Andrea in.

'Sit in that chair,' yelled one of the offices to her as their left the room.

A moment later Tapping and Yilmaz entered and sat on the two chairs opposite her.

'Where did it all go wrong for you?' asked Tapping.

'What are you talking about?' she answered back.

'You are educated, you have a good job, so why did you join the ranks of EOKA?

'I and many other Cypriots want freedom; we no longer want to be part of the British empire. This is our land. We are all freedom fighters,' she passionately said aloud.

'What freedom! EOKA advocates Enosis with Greece. Do you think Greek Cypriots will be freer under direct rule from Greece than that the British?' Interrupted Yilmaz.

Tapping glanced at Yilmaz clearly unhappy with his comment.

'Let us keep to the facts. I want to know what involvement you had in the murder of the two British soldiers near the Roman site and in the abduction of your colleagues, Mr

Megaw, Mr Catling and Mr Mustafa? We know you were part of the EOKA cell, and you tried to recruit Christos to join your group.'

Andrea just stared at Tapping.

'A British patrol unit always left the camp at Limni at the same time everyday and drove the same route. It was simple to plan the ambush. All I did was tell my group what time the patrol would pass by the Roman site,' she admitted.

'Do you not feel any remorse for the families of the two soldiers that were murdered?' asked Tapping.

Andrea then pointed a finger at Yilmaz.

'Do you feel any remorse for the family of Panayotis Michalis, the man you murdered?'

'Michalis murdered Sergeant Hasan Mustafa, one of my best friends and the uncle of Kaya Mustafa. Did you ever tell Kaya that one of your freedom fighters murdered his uncle?' responded Yilmaz.

'What was your relationship with Kaya? I hear it was intimate, but you had no second thoughts about telling your friends the exact route Kaya and his colleagues would be taking to transport the Roman coins,' pressed Tapping.

'I like Kaya but I had to choose between him and my country.'

'What would have happened to Kaya, Megaw and Catling?' asked Tapping.

'There were only supposed to take the Roman coins, but they decided to hold them hostage. I had no say in the matter, but the orders were to kill them,' admitted Andrea.

'That's enough,' Tapping said bluntly as he got up from his chair.

'What's going to happen to me?' asked Andrea.

'You will be held in a detention camp until the new governor decides what to do with all EOKA detainees.'

A crowd gathered near the water fountain in Tera. A large truck with EAC written on its side was blocking the road. Mehmet Bey was in discussion with a couple of workmen when another large truck arrived with what seemed like miles of cables in the back. Three more men jumped out of the truck cab and one of those men appeared to be the foreman, as he was holding a clip board with official papers clipped on.

'Are you in charge?' Mehmet Bey said to the man.

'Yes. My name is Takis,' confirmed the man.

Mehmet Bey produced a carbon copy piece of paper and thrust it in front of Takis.

'I have paid the deposit, and when everything is installed and the whole village has electricity I will pay the remaining balance,' stated Mehmet Bey.

Takis was somewhat overwhelmed by Mehmet Bey's direct approach. At that point the sound of a motorbike heralded the arrival of Mehmet Bey's son, Sergeant Yilmaz, who had to put his brakes on to stop his motorbike careering into the truck blocking the road. Yilmaz took off his helmet slightly confused as to what an Electricity Authority of Cyprus truck was doing in the middle of Tera.

'That is my son,' Mehmet Bey proudly informed Takis.

Yilmaz walked over to Mehmet Bey and Takis.

'What is going on here?' asked Yilmaz.

'This man and his fellow workers are going to bring electricity to Tera,' explained Mehmet Bey.

Yilmaz was taken by surprise by this development. He knew electricity was increasingly being supplied to towns and villages, but precedence had been given to Greek inhabitant villages, such as Kritou.

'Were you given orders by the British to supply electricity to Tera?' he asked Takis.

'No, Mehmet Bey here is paying for it. If a village pays the authority they jump to the top of the queue,' said Takis.

Yilmaz looked at his father wondering how the earth he would have afforded to pay for the electricity supply.

'Can I look at the paperwork?' Yilmaz asked Takis.

Takis handed him the papers.

'I will explain how it will work. There is a distribution substation that supplies electricity transmission to Kritou, and all we need to do is install lines from Kritou to this village. In a number of days the whole village will have electricity,' Takis informed father and son and the ever-increasing crowd.

'The whole village will have electricity in a few days,' Mehmet Bey proclaimed, and the crowd began to cheer and clap.

Yilmaz handed the papers back to Takis.

'Is everything in order Sergeant?'

'It seems to be.'

'Thank you, Sergeant. I'll tell my men to start immediately,' said Takis.

Yilmaz stood next to Mehmet Bey.

'Dad, where did you get the money to pay for this?'

Mehmet Bey put his arm around Yilmaz.

'Son, it was a gift from Allah. A gift ensuring the future prosperity of the village. Everyone is going to benefit. My ambition is to install a couple of electric water pumps. Could you image how much time that would save me watering all my crops? One day when you decide to leave the police force you can come back and help me farm.'

Yilmaz was incredulous to what his father was telling him.

'Dad, I have told you countless times I have no intention of being a farmer, I have no interest in it. I am going to be honest with you, I do not want to hurt your feelings, but I need to tell you the truth. There is no future for me in Cyprus, my only two options are staying in the police force or working on a farm. For me these are not attractive, nor appealing,' Yilmaz confessed to his father.

'What do you want to do, son?'

'If you had not denied me an education, I could have been at least a teacher or another professional, but all you were interested in me being was a farmer like you! I think I am smart enough to have gone to college or university, but I was never given the opportunity to prove myself,' Yilmaz said with more and more anger.

'One day all this land will be yours. You will be the wealthiest man in the village, in the whole of Baf. What else would you want?' asked Mehmet Bey.

'More than you, more than this village, and more than this Island can offer.'

Mehmet Bey shook his head unable to understand his son's feelings.

'Look, I would be happy for you to take the over the farm. I would take a back seat and you can decide how you would like to run it.'

'Dad, you know and I know that will never happen. You need to be in total control. Total control! Joining the Police force was my way of gaining some independence from you and the village, but ultimately, to gain total independence my only option would be to leave Cyprus,' replied Yilmaz.

'Where would you go?'

'I have not thought that far ahead. I will need to wait and see what happens in the next couple of years,' said Yilmaz unsure himself of what his future would look like.

Another man was hovering around the father and son. Mehmet Bey wanted to continue this heart to heart conversation with his son, a rarity, an occurrence he could not remember the last time it happened.

'Yilmaz, why don't you come round to the house tonight?' Yilmaz pondered his father's request.

'I cannot tonight but I will come round with Lutfiye and Zorlu at the weekend.'

Mehmet Bey nodded as he turned to the man who was standing next to him listening in to the conversation.

'Can I help you?' Mehmet Bey abruptly asked the man.

'Are you Mehmet Bey?'

'Yes.'

'I am from CITA.'

'CITA?' a confused Mehmet Bey said.

'He is from the telephone company,' Yilmaz confirmed to his father.

'Yes, I want a phone line installed in the village. It is a disgrace that the village has no phone. Why is it that only Greek villages have phone lines?' Mehmet Bey asked the man from the Telephone company.

'Mehmet Bey, I am just an engineer. The company tells me and my men where to go and our job is to erect telephone poles and a line.'

'I understand. I did not mean to vent my frustration at you. You're just doing your job,' Mehmet Bey said in apologetic fashion.

'Why don't you speak to that man over there? He is from the electricity company, so you can co-ordinate with him,' Yilmaz suggested as he pointed to Takis.

As the telephone man walked over to Takis, Yilmaz

tapped his father's shoulder.

'I can see you are busy. I will see you at the weekend,'

Poles were erected, cables hauled and connected. Once the main electricity power line was connected, a firm of electricians were brought in to install power to every household in the village. One morning two large trucks arrived, and Mehmet Bey was there to greet them. One of the drivers pulled open the canvas cover from the back of his truck to reveal dozens of refrigerators.

'Where do you want them?' the driver asked Mehmet Bey.

'I want every house to have one, can you also deliver one to the mosque and two to the café,' instructed Mehmet Bey.

Being provided with a fridge enabled the villagers to change their food storage and preparation habits, but the major change was the power of light. No more gaslight or candlelit rooms. Mehmet Bey was filled with a great sense of satisfaction and pride as he toured the village visiting and inspecting every house, keeping a list of any other requirements he could help with.

Ali Mustafa wiped the police badge of his deceased brother Hasan. For a moment Ali could see Hasan's smiling face, joking, and laughing together. Ali was the protective older brother who always kept an eye on Hasan while at school. Even when Hasan decided to join the police force their relationship remained close. Ali was in an old truck with two of his friends, Metin and Hussain, parked in the market square in Kritou. They were observing the comings and goings of people to the village shop and the café directly opposite. It was a Saturday night and many of the villagers would go to the café to socialise with other local inhabitants. A car stopped outside the shop and two men got out of the car. Metin, who was in the drivers' seat, nudged Ali. One of the men was limping.

'Hussain, let's go,' said Ali as he got out of the car. Hussain followed, and both men walked to the shop. They were both wearing black jackets and Ali had a peaked cap that he slightly lowered to cover his upper face. He also lifted the collars of his jacket to obscure the lower part of his face. Ali walked into the shop, and the man with the limp was at the counter talking to the shop keeper before asking for a packet of cigarettes. Ali walked up to the counter and stood next to the man, who turned to look at Ali, who smiled, turned, and gestured to Hussain to leave the shop.

'It is him. He is the EOKA gunman who tried to kill Sergeant Yilmaz at the café in Tera,' Ali told Hussain.

Ali nodded to Metin prompting him to start the truck. Ali and Hussain waited by the EOKA men's car. The two EOKA men left the shop and the one with the limp opened the packet of cigarettes, put one in his mouth, and lit it up. Ali reached into his jacket and produced a revolver. Hussain approached the men.

'Sorry, to trouble you, but do you have a spare cigarette?' asked Hussain in Greek.

The EOKA man looked at Hussain.

'Of course,' said the man who duly gave Hussain a cigarette and lit it up for him.

'Thank you. Have a good day,' said Hussain as he briskly walked away.

Ali, who was standing ten feet away, raised his hand and fired six shots at the two men. The truck driven by Metin pulled up next to the car and Ali and Hussain, who still had the cigarette in his mouth, rushed into it before Metin drove off.

'Did you get them both?' asked Metin.

'Yes, three shots each,' Ali confirmed.

Metin drove the truck to his farm that was located on the outskirts of Tera. Metin parked the truck in one of the outbuildings normally used to house cattle.

'Give me your jackets,' Metin told the other two.

Ali and Hussain handed over their identical jackets, Ali also handed over his cap.

'You better take this as well,' said Ali as he handed Metin the revolver.

Metin put the jackets and revolver in a cloth bag and all three left the building. Metin locked the door.

'I will see you later,' Ali said to the others as he got into his truck.

Hussain jumped into his tractor and waved goodbye to the others. Ali drove off but as he held the steering wheel, his hands were visibly shaking. A hot flush came over him and he begun to profusely sweat, and within a minute or so he felt wet due to the number of sweat patches on his shirt. He turned into the drive of his house and when he stopped, he put his head onto the steering wheel. Gradually his body began to calm down. The shaking stopped and so did the sweating. He climbed out of his truck and dragged his body inside the house and headed straight to the bedroom before collapsing onto his bed, the emotional strain of his action overpowering his physical strength. Images of the EOKA men flashed before Ali's eyes, shutting them tightly did not eradicate the faces, and he twisted and turned before falling asleep.

Sir Hugh Foot had been Governor of Jamaica and seemed to be well liked by the local population due to his liberal views. Therefore, his appointment as the new

Governor of Cyprus was seen by the British Government as an opportunity for Foot to negotiate with Makarios and Grivas and win over the locals. Major General Kendrew was at Nicosia airport waiting for the arrival of Foot. Kendrew, accompanied by Tapping and Yilmaz were waiting on the tarmac of the airport as the plane doors opened and Foot walked down the stairs followed by his wife. Tapping and Yilmaz were in the land rover driven by Officer Fuat. The Governor's limousine followed the land rover from the airport to the Governor's residence. Foot wanted an audience with Kendrew and Major Scott while Tapping and Yilmaz waited outside.

'Gentlemen, reviewing the number of EOKA members we have detained. I have decided that anyone who has been interned for being a suspected member and has not actually been convicted of a criminal offence should be released with immediate effect. I think we need to move on from this heavy-handed policing approach,' Foot instructed.

'Understood Sir Hugh. That is probably a wise move,' said Kendrew.

Foot put down one document on his desk and picked up another.

'Major Scott, I have read your report and I marked a couple of points. The most worrying for me is the rise of the number of incidences of EOKA killing Turkish Cypriots and vice versa.'

'Well, there was an incident a day or so ago. Two Greek Cypriots, both EOKA suspects I must add, were gunned down in a village that has had several inter-communal incidents. We have not tracked down the gunman but believe he was a Turkish Cypriot,' Scott reported.

'I have also highlighted the number of Greek-on-Greek

killings,' noted Foot.

'These are EOKA killing Greek Cypriot civilians mainly due the belief that they have spoken to the police or those who actively disagree with Grivas' politics,' confirmed Scott.

'I am not too worried about that aspect, but the inter-communal killings are a major concern,' replied Foot.

Room III at the museum in Nicosia had been newly re-decorated. It was one of fourteen rooms, and it was dedicated to antiquities from the middle of the bronze age to the Roman period. The exhibited objects consisted of local ceramic pottery, but on this day a new display table had been assembled and a small plaque plate set in the middle of the table. ROMAN AUREUS COINS FROM THE PERIOD OF RULE OF HADRIAN C. 123 AD.

The curator of the museum delicately placed ten coins in the middle of the display. Kaya was observing from behind the curator and helped lift the glass case that was placed on the display cabinet.

'Can I take a photograph please?' asked the reporter from the Cyprus Mail.

Kaya and the curator stood either side of the display as a few photos were taken.

'When will the article appear in the paper?' Kaya asked the reporter.

'It will be in the weekend edition, covered in our arts and entertainment section,' the reporter confirmed.

'One question I would like to ask is, where is the rest of coins?' asked the reporter.

'They have been locked away in the museum vaults,' Kaya informed him.

The reporter took one last close-up photo of the coins before leaving. A staff member entered the room.

'Kaya, Mr Megaw would like to see you in his office.'

Mr Megaw was shuffling pieces of papers on his desk when Kaya entered.

'How is the new display looking?' Megaw asked him.

'I am really proud of it. The Cyprus Mail is printing an article about the coins going on display at the weekend. Hopefully, that would lead to an increase in admissions,' Kaya informed him.

'That is good. Anyway the reason I want to talk to you is about a letter I received from Professor Alwright at Cambridge,' said Megaw as he picked up the letter.

'What is the letter about?' asked a surprised and slightly confused Kaya.

'The Professor informs me that the department of archaeology has a vacancy for a research position at the university that could lead to a PhD. He continues by saying that the ideal candidate for this role would be you,' Megaw says pointing at Kaya.

'I do not know what to say. Is the research role a paid position?'

Megaw handed the letter to Kaya who took it like he was going to devour it. After reading the letter he handed back to Megaw.

'What are your thoughts?' asked Megaw.

'In my last year at Cambridge, Professor Alwright kept recommending that I should stay on at the university. But I just do not know. My first instinct is to apply for it, as this is a once in a lifetime opportune and considering everything that has happening here this seems to be an escape route. So, I really have to consider it.'

'Kaya, it is your choice I will support whatever you decide, but there is something I need to tell you. I have been Director here since 1935, I love the island, but if Cyprus gains independence in the next couple of years, then I probably will have to leave the museum. Mr Catling would also probably leave his role. When this happens, the likelihood is that the Director and Head of the Archaeological Survey Branch would be Cypriots. I personally feel that if you decide to stay at the museum, you are eminently qualified, and with a few years added experience you would be a leading candidate for either position,' Megaw explained.

Megaw's comments took Kaya by surprise.

'I would never have considered what you have said as an option. When I graduated from Cambridge the limit of my only ambition was to find a role on an excavation, so I was over the moon when I was offered a position here, said Kaya.

'What is your ambition, Kaya?' asked Megaw.

'I just want to travel the World discovering long lost civilizations, but Cyprus has such a rich and diverse history, I could spend a lifetime excavating sites on the Island. So, my loyalties are therefore divided.'

'I would say it is a good dilemma to have. Your future is assured, so whichever direction you decide to go would ultimately be the correct one,' said Megaw.

'It is one for me to ponder on for a while,' Kaya told him.

Once the entrance door was opened a flock of people entered all anticipating seeing the newly discovered Roman coins. Kaya walked into Room III to see a mass of people huddled around the cabinet displaying the coins.

'Where is the rest of them?' one of the people asked.

'I heard they found hundreds of coins,' said another.

Kaya smiled to himself as he looked at his watch and

realised he was running late for his rendezvous. After grabbing his jacket from the staff room, he exited the museum from the staff entrance at the back, the bells from the nearby church rang twelve times to indicate to Kaya that he was late. The speediness of his walking was negated by the throng of people he had to navigate past. He brushed past a group of four British soldiers, who looked at him suspiciously. He dared not look back just in case the soldiers called him back or asked him to stop. Finally, he reached his destination, a Café located in a cul-da-sac off Ledra Street. Entering the café, he was surprised by its bustling nature.

'Can I help you?' one of the waitresses asked him.

'I am meeting someone here.'

The number of full tables made it difficult for Kaya to see.

'Maybe try downstairs,' suggested the waitress.

Kaya walked down the narrow stairs to the basement where it was far less busy. He smiled and walked over to the table.

'Hello Kaya.'

Seated there was Andrea. This was the first time he had seen her since he was abducted by the EOKA men and there was a certain amount of awkwardness. She stood up and initiated a kiss on both cheeks. Kaya sat down.

'How have you been?' Kaya asked her.

'The last few weeks haven't been the best weeks of my life I must say. I was detained in an internment camp and then lost my job at the museum.'

She was interrupted by the waitress walking over to their table.

'What can I get you?' asked the Waitress.

'I am not really that hungry. Can I just get a coffee please?' said Andrea.

'I'm not hungry either. I will have a coffee as well.'

'Are you sure you do not want anything to eat?' the waitress asked again.

'No!' Andrea and Kaya said in unison.

The waitress walked away muttering under her breath.

'So, how have you been?' Andrea asked Kaya.

'I am just contemplating my future and whether to stay at the museum or return to Cambridge. What would you do if you were in my shoes?'

'If you asked me that question a few weeks ago, I would have said to stay in Cyprus and stay at the museum. My answer today would be to go to England, but my current predicament is different from yours.'

'I understand. I also wanted to ask you a couple a questions. Did you know that Mr Megaw, Mr Catling, and I were going to be abducted by your comrades? And did you know what they intended to do with us?' he asked with a degree of discomfort.

Andrea's eyes began to fill up with tears as the pair stared intensely at each other.

'No. I did tell them when we were departing and the route, but the plan was only to take the coins.'

'If you had known their true intentions, would you have gone through with this plan?' he asked.

'No, when they put all three of you in the back of the truck, I pleaded with them not to take you, but they said Digenis had ordered them to kidnap you,' she explained.

'Do you know what our fate would have been if we had not been rescued?'

'Digenis had ordered his men to have you killed. I was summoned by him and had to be escorted to his hideout. I told him that I did not want anything else to do with EOKA, but he insisted that once you become a member there is no way to leave. I had no choice, as I do not care about me, but I do not want my family to suffer. When the police arrested me, I was glad. This way I could escape the clutches of EOKA. I have been staying with friends since my release.'

'Why did you want to meet with me?' he asked.

'Kaya, I loved you. I cannot just forget you, forget everything that happened between us,' she said as tears began to flow down her cheeks.

'I loved you, but then you betrayed me. I think about you every second of the day, but you broke my heart.'

Andrea started sobbing and this prompted Kaya to take out and hand her a handkerchief. She dabbed her tears from her face and as she went to give the handkerchief back Kaya held both her hands. The waitress brought them their coffee and placed the cups and two glasses of water in front of them.

'I am sorry, I didn't mean to hurt you. I was just following instructions,' she admitted.

'I must be honest with you I had my suspicions. When we were in Polis I saw you outside the post office with a man I recognized as a EOKA gunman.'

Andrea nodded.

'Why didn't you tell anybody?' she asked.

'I was in love with you. How could I throw it all away? My uncle was killed by EOKA, so my mind and heart were torn. In reality I had to choose between my family and you, and I chose you,' admitted Kaya.

Two men from the table behind were eavesdropping on Kaya's and Anderea's conversation.

'I am sorry Kaya, I wish I never got involved with them. I do not know what else I can say. Holding your hand like this proves that I still have feelings for you. What about you? What do you feel? Do you still have feelings for me?' she asked overwhelming Kaya with these questions.

'Of course, I still have feelings for you. But maybe not the same feelings I had when we first got together.'

'Do you think you could rekindle those feelings we initially had?' she asked.

Kaya gazed at her realizing that she looked even more beautiful now than she did when he first met her.

'What are you saying? Do you still want to continue having a relationship with me?' he asked her.

'If you can forgive me for being involved in EOKA and the consequences that has had on you and your family, then my answer is yes. I would love to go on another excavation with you.'

'If we keep uncovering treasures like the Roman coins I would excavate every day of the week, and most importantly I would like to excavate every day with you,' responded Kaya as he held Andrea's hand tighter.

'That would be my idea of utopia,' she said with a wide smile.

'Excavating every day or being with me every day?'

'Both,' she said giggling.

'Who knows, if I stay with the Museum and you come back, and your utopian dream may be achieved. There are so many sites on the Island the archeological branch could start excavating. What do you think of that idea? In time you can apply for your old job back.'

'Realistically, you're talking about a long time in the future and I'm not sure if I can wait that long,' she commented.

'I have a proposal. You can always come and work with me unofficially?'

She smiled at Kaya's well-meaning intentions.

'Are you going to stay in Tera?' asked Andrea.

'For the time being. The village has completely changed, I mean changed for the good. Every house now has electricity. That was like a godsend. It also has two telephones, one in the café and one in Mehmet Bey's house,' he informed her.

'How is Mehmet Bey? It seems he has put the gold coins to use,' she said somewhat sarcastically.

'He is a good man, and he has done good for the village so I for one do not begrudge him and apart from you and me no one else knows about the coins he took.'

'You are right he is a good man and I have not and will not tell another soul,' she said.

Kaya finished off his coffee.

'This will keep me alert this afternoon. Where is your friend's house,' he asked her.

'Her house is on the outskirts of Nicosia. She is an old college friend of mine she also studied at Athens University.'

'Are you going to be looking for another job?'

'I have an interview at a printing company next week. It is a clerical role, but it will do for the time being,' she said.

'Since you are based here do you want to meet again for lunch?' Kaya asked her.

'I would love to,' Andrea said without hesitation.

'How about tomorrow? Asked Kaya.

'Well, I don't have any plans. So, yes.'

'I will have a bit longer for lunch as Mr Megaw and Mr Catling are on a site visit tomorrow. Now that they have closed the Roman camp excavation site, I will be based at the museum for the time being. I find it dead boring; I would much rather be out in the field excavating.'

'Maybe we can go for something to eat,' suggested Andrea.

'That sounds like a very good idea to me,' said Kaya with a big wide smile.

The café was beginning to empty, and Kaya looked at his watch.

'Let me pay for the coffees,' he said as he gesticulated to the waitress to bring over the bill.

'Thank you. Where do you want to meet tomorrow?' she asked.

'How about Michael's place? I have never been, but friends tell me the food there is pretty good,' he suggested.

'Good choice, their kleftiko with rice is delicious.'

'That is a date. Twelve o'clock tomorrow outside Michael's place.'

The waitress brought the bill to the table, which Kaya promptly paid.

'Shall we go?' said Kaya.

The pair got up form the table and walked upstairs. The upstairs was empty apart from two people sat at a table.

'Are you going to your friends flat?' he asked.

'I might do some window shopping down Ledra Street. I don't have any money, but it is always good to see something you like and hope you can save up to buy it one day,' Andrea said.

'Yes, I have those dreams every night. I always want things I cannot have now, but that is it, cannot have now. My goal is to get to a position life where you can have most things, if not everything, you want.'

'I love that ideology. I think that is want I will aim for,' she said with a huge smile on her face.

'Well, it is goodbye until tomorrow,' said Kaya as he embraced Andrea.

They gazed into each other's eyes before engaging in a passionate kiss.

'I cannot wait until tomorrow,' Andrea confessed.

'Nor can I,' responded Kaya.

Their parting seemed to take an eternity.

'See you tomorrow,' said Andrea.

'Will do,' he replied.

Kaya wandered down the street in no particular hurry to get back to the museum. He exuded the widest grin in Nicosia. People stared at him as they passed him by, but he was undeterred, it was the happiest he had been for a while, and he wanted to show the whole World how happy he was. As he turned into Museum Street, for a second or two everything turned silent, it was as though someone had turned the volume down on the radio. No sound of car engines on the road, no sound of people's voices on the pavements just pure silence. Then the sound of a gun shot rang out cutting the silence asunder, followed by a second shot. Kaya stopped in his tracks; screams followed close behind the gunshot sound. Instinct seemed to kick in, Kaya turned and ran back towards Ledra Street. A crowd had gathered just outside a jewelry shop, and Kaya could hear thumping boots of four British soldiers running to the scene. The crowd parted as the soldiers reached the scene and Kaya could see the body of a young woman on the ground, as he edged closer, it gradually dawned on him that the woman lying on the ground was Andrea. Venturing forward he got to the point that he was standing over her.

'Get back!' shouted a British Soldier at Kaya.

Kaya ignored his orders and stood there looking at Andrea.

'I said stand back,' the British soldier barked at Kaya pointing his rifle to Kaya's midriff.

'I know this woman,' said Kaya to the soldier.

'Are you a relative?' the soldier asked in a much calmer voice.

'No, I used to work with her.'

A man burst through the crowd.

'Let me through I'm a Doctor,' he said as he knelt down to attend to her.

Kaya stood stone cold unable to move. A police car arrived followed by an ambulance. The police officers began to tell the people crowded around to move on. The ambulance men knelt next to the Doctor. A few minutes later, one of the ambulance men stood up and walked to the back of the ambulance. Kaya's eyes were transfixed on him and as he returned, he was carrying a blanket. Kaya's heart rate dropped and everything all around him seemed to move in slow motion. The Doctor stood up and nodded to the ambulance man who placed the blanket over Andrea's body. The Doctor looked at Kaya and shook his head and at that point Kaya's heartbeat shot up making everything speed up. The soldier started speaking, but to Kaya, what he was saying sounded gibberish. Kaya turned and walked away, unable to comprehend what he had just seen. Kaya reached the museum, slumped down onto the steps and began to sob. One of museum employees saw Kaya and rushed inside. Minutes later Mr Megaw came out.

'Kaya, what has happened?'

Kaya wiped away his tears with the sleeve of his jacket and looked up to Megaw.

'Andrea is dead.'

Megaw helped him up and escorted him into the museum.

Evening was setting in and Ali was sat outside in the back yard of the house. A glass and a bottle of brandy were next to him. Kaya drove into the drive and parked inside. Ali lifted his hand up to greet his son. Kaya sluggishly got out of his seat and Ali immediately sensed there was something not quite right.

'Kaya, come here.'

Kaya reluctantly walked over to Ali.

'What's wrong, son?'

Fumes from the brandy hit Kaya full in the face.

'How much have you drunk?'

'Not enough,' came Ali's reply.

'Where is Mum?' asked Kaya.

'She has gone to Arodes with your aunt. Tell me what has happened?'

'Andrea is dead.'

'What! How!'

'Someone shot her this afternoon in Ledra Street.'

Ali stood up.

'Sit down,' Ali told Kaya as he headed inside the house.

Kaya slumped down in the chair with his bloodshot eyes bulging out. The day's events had left him physically and emotionally drained. Ali came back out holding another bottle of brandy and a glass. He poured a full glass of brandy in front of Kaya and pulled up a chair, before pouring himself a glass.

'You were fond of her,' said Ali.

'I think I loved her,' Kaya said as he drunk the brandy.

Ali shook his head to disagree with Kaya's comment.

'She was pretty, I would have to admit that, but to me she was a rose on the outside and a bed of thorns on the inside.'

'What do you mean?' said Kaya in an angry tone.

Ali drunk his glass of brandy and poured himself some more.

'What do I mean? I mean she was a member of EOKA. These people are not only the enemies of the British but also enemies of all Turkish Cypriots. They killed my brother and I will never forgive them,' Ali said with passion with a slight slur in his speech.

'Andrea had nothing to do with Uncle Hasan's death. She gave her forgiveness to me.'

'Forgiveness will not bring your uncle back. Anyway, who murdered Andrea?' questioned Ali.

'I don't know. People at the scene said it was a lone gunman.'

'I will tell you who killed her. EOKA. They even kill their own people. These people are animals, and we will hunt them down. We got two of them the other day,' Ali blurted out as he carried on drinking.

'I don't understand you. Which two did you get the other day?' asked a confused Kaya.

Ali pretended to shoot a gun with his hand. Kaya stood up.

'Did you have anything to do with the two men who were shot in Kritou?'

'They were not just two men. Did I have anything to do with it? I was the one who shot them,' Ali said proudly.

'No!' screamed Kaya.

Ali stood up.

'Son, I was petrified. After I shot them, I started to shake and sweat for at least an hour afterwards. I could not sleep that night all I kept seeing were blood-soaked bodies. I was an evil man for killing another human being. Today, I looked at myself in the mirror and said I was justified in my actions, and I will shout out so the whole world could hear that I would do it again.'

'Dad, what is going to happen if the police find out it was you? Jail... you could spend the rest of life in prison. What do you think it's going to do to Mum? She will never recover from the trauma,' Kaya shouted at Ali.

'So be it,' responded Ali.

'Is that all you have to say, so be it? Dad you are

murderer, in fact, you are a double murderer.'

Ali sat back down and poured himself another brandy and poured some into Kaya's glass.

Silence ensued. Kaya sat down and continued drinking.

'I don't think I can stay here any longer,' said Kaya.

'This house?' said Ali.

'This house, this village, this island. I need to get away.'

Ali stood up and walked to the back door and turned on a light switch and the backyard lit up.

'We have light!' Ali yelled throwing both arms in the air.

Kaya gave his dad a hard stare and shook his head. Ali walked back to the table almost stumbling on the way.

'Are you still grieving over that EOKA girl?'

'Her name was Andrea,' Kaya answered back.

'She deserved to die,' Ali said quietly.

'What did you say?' shouted Kaya.

'You heard me very well, she deserved to die, even EOKA thought she was a traitor that's why they had her killed.'

Kaya stood up and threw his glass at the wall.

'Sorry dad, but I need to go.'

Kaya stormed out the side of the house to his car. Ali went after him.

'Where are you going?

Kaya opened the car door and turned back to Ali.

'I need some time on my own,' said Kaya before getting into his car and driving off.

BANG! Kaya was startled by the sound of banging. Once he came to his senses and realized he had been asleep in his car, he looked out of the windows. He could see three British surrounding his car. One of the soldiers was gesticulating to him to wind down his car window, which he did.

'Get out of the car!' the soldier aggressively shouted.

Kaya gingerly got out the car.

'What are you doing here?' shouted the aggressive soldier.

Kaya turned around to get his bearings and started to laugh.

'Do you think this is funny?'

Kaya then pointed to the museum.

'I work there,' said Kaya with a big grin on his face.

His car was parked right by the entrance gate to the museum.

'Prove it?' the aggressive soldier asked.

'My pass is in the glove compartment of my car,' Kaya said.

'Move away from the car.'

Kaya stepped onto the pavement and next to the entrance gate.

The soldier walked round to the front passenger side and opened door and open the glove compartment and took out Kaya's pass.

'Kaya Mustafa,' the soldier said out loud.

'That's me.'

'You should not be parked here,' the soldier told Kaya.

'I know. Let me drive it into the car park.'

The soldiers walked away. Kaya got back into his car to find the car keys still in the ignition. He started the car and slowly drove it into the museum car park. Confirmation of how early it was, was provided by the staff entrance door still being locked. He sat down and rested his head on the door.

'Hello!'

Kaya opened his eyes and looked up to see the museum caretaker standing over him.

'Good morning. I have an early start,' Kaya explained as he stood to his feet.

As soon as the caretaker opened the door Kaya briskly made his way to the staff toilets. After he emerged from the toilet cubicle, he stared at himself in the mirror, the main features that stood for him were his unkempt hair, bleary eyes and unshaven complexion. He doused himself in cold water from the tap, tried to fix his hair and washed out his mouth in an attempt to extinguish the fumes of the brandy. He was the first person to go into the staff room and made himself a large mug of Turkish coffee. Mr Megaw entered the staff room.

'What are you doing here so early?' asked Megaw.

'Can I speak to you when you have a minute?' said Kaya.

'Come to my office with me.'

Megaw made himself a cup of tea and pair walked to his office.

'If you do not mind me saying, you look slightly worse for wear,' Megaw said to Kaya.

'Yes, I didn't sleep too well last night.'

They entered Megaw's office and sat down.

'I have made my decision. I want to apply for the position at Cambridge. I do not want to stay in Cyprus any longer,' Kaya told Megaw.

'Are you a hundred percent certain this is the decision you would like to make?' Megaw double checked.

'One hundred percent,' confirmed Kaya.

Megaw finished his cup of tea.

'I will speak to Professor Alwright. I am sure he will be pleased. I will speak to him this afternoon, I will let you know what he says,' Megaw confirmed.

'Thank you.'

'Why don't you have the day off. Go home and get some rest. We can talk again tomorrow morning,' suggested Megaw.

'I will sir. Thank you again.'

The museum staff began to arrive for work as Kaya left. The last twenty four hours had left him in a daze. After locating his car, he sat in there to reflect on life. Kaya was finding it difficult to erase the constant image of Andrea from his mind, but he knew that he had to move on and maybe moving to England would give him the opportunity to do so. Separation from his family would be the most difficult aspect of leaving but pondering on his father's action, he asked himself if he could ever look into his father's eyes with the same level of respect a son should have for his father. Thoughts circulated through his mind and after an hour sat in his car, he sub-consciously nodded to himself, clearer in his mind the next steps he had to take but it also helped cement the decision on his future. He drove off out of the city of Nicosia and into a new direction of his life.

Printed in Great Britain
by Amazon